DUST STORM

JASON TRAPP BOOK 9

JACK SLATER

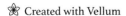

1

D iyala Governate, Iraq.
2007.

THE RAM COLLIDED with the decrepit, sun-bleached wooden door with enough force to smash it off its hinges. It flew backward in a hail of splinters that appeared as ghostly flashes through the green view cast by the night vision goggles.

"Sikorski, breach!" Jason Trapp shouted at the soldier in front of him, detecting a hint of wariness in the Ranger probably even before the kid himself did. He slapped the back of his helmet for emphasis.

The private entered the breached doorway, pressing his back against the wall to the right and sliding across with his carbine raised and aimed in the opposite direction. Trapp's view opened up the second Sikorski was inside, and he followed on muscle memory alone, sticking to the wall on the left and sidestepping along its full course. The rifle in his hands barely quivered despite the flood of adrenaline coursing through his veins.

"Clear!" Sikorski called at about the same time as Trapp came to that conclusion himself. The beams of two IR lasers swept across the room, visible only through their NVGs. Two more added to the light show as the final members of the Ranger fire team entered the isolated Iraqi farmhouse. Both men situated themselves in controlling positions over the internal doorway that was the only other entry point to the room they had just breached. Like Trapp and Sikorski, their actions were both textbook and deeply ingrained.

"Chambers, door," he snapped, his chest straining for breath. The desert heat was concentrated by the pounds of gear attached to his frame and locked in by his body armor. Sweat trickled down his forehead and burned his eyes.

He raised his carbine's muzzle as the Army specialist crossed his path, then lowered it again the second he was through. The delay pained him—successful building clearance operations relied on speed and the shock it caused the enemy.

Slow is smooth, smooth is fast.

The mantra was calming, as was the knowledge that barely a couple of seconds had elapsed since they'd burst into the farmhouse. He approached the next door along with the remainder of the members of his fire team, all remaining behind the cover of the thick mud-brick walls as Chambers positioned himself to the right of the doorway.

"Punch it," Trapp muttered. He sucked in a breath, steadied himself, and prepared for a hail of bullets to fly through the open doorway. He imagined a grenade bouncing through the second it swung open, detonating, his friends covered in blood.

Chambers twisted his wrist and drew the door back in the same motion. From opposite sides of the doorway, Trapp and Sikorski peered in, sweeping the secondary room with their weapons.

"Clear." Both men's voices rang out at the same time, equally gruff and hoarse from the dust that hung in the air.

Behind the door lay a hallway with two doors on either side which stretched out about ten yards before twisting into a sharp left, following the L-shaped layout of the farmhouse building. Trapp wished he had a set of blueprints. But the last few months had taught him that Iraqi construction workers didn't exactly understand the concept of standardization. Every home they assaulted was different from the last. Any doorway, nook, or cranny could—and often did—harbor an insurgent armed with both a weapon and a burning desire to expel the American invaders.

"Move, move," Trapp hissed, though the command was redundant. Behind him, he heard the boots of a second fire team thundering into the farmhouse to cover their six.

"Taking first left," Sikorski muttered, indicating he was going to hit the first of the four doorways. "You throw the flasher."

"Copy," Trapp replied, his breath heavy in his ears.

The two men positioned themselves much like they had before, except with Sikorski in Chambers' role and the others covering the remainder of the hallway. Terse statements carried from the second fire team, now filing into the hallway. Trapp blocked out the distraction as he unclipped an M84 flashbang grenade from his utility belt, pulled the pin, and signaled to Sikorski that he was ready.

"Breaching," Sikorski said, his voice coming out in a pubescent squeak.

As the Polish-American Ranger drew the door back, Trapp tossed the stun grenade inside. Sikorski slammed the door shut once more, and all four men covered their ears and eyes. Even so, the detonation rocked through the small group, the rickety wooden door doing little to stem the waves of sound and pressure.

Sikorski opened the door, and Trapp swept the interior with the IR flashlight clipped to the end of his carbine, knowing that as he did so, one of the two other Rangers was doing the same on the other side. They were a well-oiled team—had to be to execute missions like this night after night.

"It's a fucking closet." He grinned, the humor acting as a pressure release for the strain he was under as fire team leader before grim seriousness reasserted itself. "Next one. Go."

Chambers switched easily into his earlier position, pulling the door on the other side open so the fourth member of the team, Eddie Muniz, could toss a flashbang inside. The door closed. The grenade detonated. Chambers yanked the handle back open, and Sikorski and Trapp leaned in.

"Gun!" Sikorski called, shouting over the sound of gunfire. The muzzle flash was impossibly bright through Trapp's night vision goggles, the room hazy from the residual. He squeezed the trigger twice, three times, putting all three rounds through the bad guy's chest.

It was overkill. Before calling out his warning, Sikorski had done the same thing. The insurgent stumbled backwards, tripped over a piece of furniture, and collapsed to the deck.

Laser beams swept the room. No further targets presented themselves. "Clear!"

The next two doorways were empty. One of Trapp's four Rangers took a knee, covering the end of the hallway with his carbine as the rest of the team swept the rooms inside. Once more, the sound of boots followed them as the second fire team mopped up behind.

Trapp couldn't allow himself the time to process the fact that he'd just helped kill a man. All that mattered right now was the safety of his soldiers and successfully executing the mission. Sweat trickled down his brow. Again. He mopped it with the back of his hand.

Again.

"Let's keep moving," he said, his throat raw from exertion.

He knew that at this very moment, another squad of Rangers was assaulting the farmhouse from the opposite side. The aim with any building clearance op was to paralyze the defenders through the use of surprise, noise, and overwhelming force. The more doorways and windows you could enter simultaneously, the less the bad guys knew where to turn. The risk in a building like this was that you didn't know how far friendly forces had made it inside. Around any corner, you could meet friend or foe, and the split second it took to work out which was which could cost a life.

Sikorski and Chambers took the right-hand wall and filed steadily forward in a low crouch. Recognizing this, he and Muniz instinctively took the left.

"Now," Trapp called the second all four men were in position. He thought he saw a grimace on Sikorski's face as the lead man threw himself into danger from the relative safety of the covering wall.

Light flashed through his goggles from the other side of the L as half a dozen gunshots rang out from the wrong direction. Sikorski went down hard. Trapp swiveled around the corner of the wall, his finger already depressing the trigger of his carbine, but about half a pound of pressure away from actually firing a shot. The laser swept across an empty space. A door slammed shut ahead of him.

"I'm good," Sikorski called out, stifling a groan. "Took a round to the chest. The plate stopped it."

Trapp jogged forward. Chambers took the right-hand side of the door, he the left. He nodded, and the soldier pulled open the door. This time he didn't bother with a flashbang. He leaned inside and scanned the room for hostiles.

No, not a room. A stairwell, leading down. Had to be to a basement. Unusual in this region, given the rocky desert ground. He heard the cries of friendlies not too far away as they cleared the capacious farmhouse from the opposite side. He was pretty sure from the tone that the only bad guys left were right below him.

"Chambers, on me," he said, peering into the darkness.

The insurgent's heavy tread echoed from the bottom of the stairs. He caught a flash of movement through his goggles as his target disappeared into the basement, jerking back behind cover for an instant in anticipation of a gunshot that never came. He sprang back around the doorpost and fired two tight bursts of his own to keep the guy pegged back.

"Let's go."

Trapp took the stairs two at a time, mentally preparing himself to ditch the night vision aids at any moment. His enemy was unlikely to have them, which meant the man was presently operating blind. It was three in the morning, and this deep into Diyala Governorate, few people had access to electric light. But even a flashlight could easily blind him once the goggles amped up the glow they emitted several thousand times. The comforting thud of Chambers' boots on the wooden steps behind him followed him down.

After swinging around a thick wooden post that appeared to support the floor above, he was presented with a cramped basement. His IR flashlight cast a pool of invisible illumination wherever he pointed his carbine. The space was filled with boxes that were stacked against every wall. Some were wood, others metal. All military. It was a weapons cache, just like the intelligence analysts had said.

But where the hell was the insurgent?

Two muzzle flashes lit up the room. The gunshots were wayward, tearing chunks of wood out of the floorboards above. Trapp pivoted toward the source and fired three of his own back, knowing as he pulled the trigger that he wouldn't hit a damn thing. He just wanted to keep the tango's head down. His ears rang from the trauma of the repeated gunshots and explosions.

"I don't see him," Chambers called out. His voice was strangled from exertion, and his heavy panting breaths filled the cramped room.

"Me neither," Trapp replied grimly. He stepped forward, the other Ranger moving in sync as they covered each other. He heard a scuffling ahead of him, then a heavy wooden thud. One of the ammunition crates in front of him shifted a few inches and threatened to topple over.

"What the fuck is he doing?"

"Put your hands up!" Trapp called out, mentally cursing the Iraqi interpreter who was supposed to follow close behind. As usual, the guy was missing in action. He just had to hope the bad guy had watched enough Hollywood B-movies to catch the gist of his commands. "Drop your weapon and you get to live."

More scuffling but no reply. Trapp chewed the inside of his lip. He didn't know what was happening up there, and he didn't like the unknown. He made the split-second decision to end this himself.

"Cover me," he instructed Chambers.

"Roger" came the reply.

Trapp weaved through the haphazardly placed ammunition crates, just hoping that none of them was rigged to blow. He was pretty sure a sweep of his flashlight had revealed a stack of artillery shells in the process of being rigged up as IEDs. This was the kind of place you didn't want firearms going off and bullets ricocheting in every direction.

Unfortunately, that was kind of out of his hands.

The basement was only a few yards across. It took him a matter of seconds to close the distance. He brought his carbine down as he crested the final row of crates, pressuring the trigger as he prepared to open fire.

But the insurgent was gone.

Trapp blinked stupidly. Behind the stack of crates, a hole gaped in the wall. It had been covered by a metal trapdoor that now lay messily to one side, revealing a narrow tunnel. The strap of the bad guy's AK had gotten tangled with the chain, and he'd left it behind as he attempted to flee.

He doubted that the guy had had the foresight to pick up a sidearm amid the panic of a night assault on this out-of-the-way compound. His brain computed as a near-certainty that the insurgent was now unarmed.

So he went in after him.

C amp Anaconda.

TRAPP JOGGED ALONE toward the tall concrete walls surrounding the HQ of Joint Special Operations Command's Task Force Center in Logistical Support Area Anaconda. Even in his head, it was a prize heifer of a military acronym. By the time he arrived at the entrance gate, Sikorski had caught up with him.

"You're one crazy motherfucker, you know that?" he said by way of introduction.

"It's 'You're one crazy motherfucker, you know that, *Sergeant,*'" Trapp shot back with an easy grin.

Sikorski mockingly clicked his heels. "Yes sir, no sir. So you heard?"

"Heard what?" Trapp replied, fishing in the pockets of his tan combat fatigues for his entrance badge.

"We hit the jackpot. Not sure exactly what, but the colonel's handling this one personally. Bad news is the CAG boys are sniffing around. Guess they want all the glory like always."

CAG was yet another military acronym in a sea of them. It stood for Combat Applications Group, an obscure term for the organization the rest of the world knew as Delta Force. Trapp's own unit, the 75th Ranger Regiment, worked closely with Delta as part of Task Force Center—the special ops grouping assigned to the Baghdad area.

"What glory?" Trapp asked, lowering his voice momentarily as they passed through the security checkpoint. The MP behind the desk scanned his badge and buzzed him through the gate.

"I guess that's what we're here to find out," Sikorski said.

Over the past two years, Task Force Center had settled into an easy rhythm as part of JSOC's contribution to ending the Iraqi Civil War. This was already Trapp's second six-month deployment at Camp Anaconda. During that time, JSOC had invented a new set of tactics for hunting high-value targets and rolling up the insurgent networks they commanded.

Instead of spending weeks planning each operation, hitting a target, and then rolling out without a second thought, the new model emphasized the value of close collaboration between Special Operations units and the intelligence outfits that fed them.

Trapp's fire team now geared up for an operation three, four, sometimes even five nights a week. They would hit a target on a Monday, capture the insurgents inside alive if possible or carry away all intelligence materials if not. While the operators slept, interrogators and intelligence analysts would spend the day drawing up a new mission based on the previous night's work. By Tuesday night, Trapp was usually on a Blackhawk with his carbine clipped to his plate carrier.

Just another day in paradise.

"But you must've heard something," Trapp said as they walked toward the briefing center. "You look like a kid on Halloween."

"I don't like candy," Sikorski said with a mock-serious expression. "But I like killing jihadis. All I heard is something's got the colonel real exercised. And we were the only op on the board last night. So my deduction, Watson, is that we had something to do with it."

Trapp elbowed his friend as they stepped through the automatic glass doors that led into the operations complex to be greeted by a freezing blast of air conditioning, a pleasant contrast to the dry desert heat.

"I guess you were right," he murmured, catching sight of an unremarkable man with a thick beard wearing civilian hiking gear and a pair of Oakley shades resting on top of his head heading in the same direction. Unlike both he and Sikorski, who were attired in their army-issued fatigues, Delta operators made a habit of eschewing wearing anything as undignified as the uniform of the country they served.

His name was Breyer, Trapp recalled. They'd only briefly met, though something about the man had rubbed him the wrong way. Most of the Delta guys wore an air of arrogance like aftershave. His was just particularly fragrant.

The briefing room was populated by a roughly even mix of uniformed Army personnel and casually—yet uniformly—dressed Delta boys and OGA types. Trapp and Sikorski entered and eyed up seats toward the back.

Captain Myers, the company commander, was at the front of the room. His camouflage shirt sleeves were rolled up to just above the elbows, and he had a thick moustache over his lip—supposedly in the name of cultural sensitivity. Though since his primary job involved sitting in an air-conditioned headquarters building and ordering his men to kick down the doors of locals in the middle of the night, all it brought to mind for Trapp was the story of the kid sticking his finger in a hole in the dike.

He clapped his hands slowly as Trapp, Sikorski, and now Chambers took their seats. "Congratulations, gentlemen. Sterling work last night."

Trapp kept his face impassive. A couple of the Delta operators shifted in their seats to eye up the recipients of such praise. Breyer was one of them. He didn't look too impressed.

"One last thing before we start," Myers said, surveying his men's faces individually in turn, seeming to consider who he intended to stop on. "Sergeant Trapp—when was the last time you sat in on an interrogation?"

Trapp flushed. One of the things that made Task Force Center's approach to combating the militant threat so lethal and clinical was the close integration of intelligence teams with the shooters they fed. Part of that involved men like him being present for interrogation sessions, and damn the need for sleep. "A few days, sir, I guess."

"Do I need to check the logs?"

"Maybe a week."

"We'll split the difference at two, Sergeant." Myers grinned. "Either way, it's not good enough. I know you're tired. I'm tired. We're all damn tired. I want to go home and see my wife. But as long as we are here in the sandbox, we do as the colonel wants. The colonel is God. His wishes are our Ten Commandments, understood?"

Trapp inclined his head. From behind him, he heard a grunted series of assents from his fellow Rangers. "Yes, sir."

"So I don't need to engrave them on stone tablets?"

"No sir. I'll attend the next one."

"And the one after that?"

"And the one after that, sir. Every day until the job is done."

"Every night until the job is done," Myers repeated, slapping his palms together at the end of each word to accentuate his point. "That's what it will take. And that's it from me."

He gestured to a lieutenant from the battalion's S2 Intelligence section and took a seat. Casey, Trapp recalled his name as. Or thought he did. He was a little too far away to make out the name badge on the man's breast.

The lieutenant leaned over the desk in front of them and hit a button on a computer keyboard. Behind the briefing table, a large projector flashed into life, at first displaying a blue screen before the device warmed up and the familiar outline of a PowerPoint presentation came into view. It was a little-known fact in the outside world that the Army—hell, the whole US military—couldn't function without its access keys for Microsoft Office.

More's the pity, Trapp thought. He'd sat through more briefings than he cared to remember. Most of them were interminably dull, hours of chaff that you had to sit through just in case one grain of wheat saved your life.

Another keystroke rang out in the suddenly quiet briefing room, and a booking photograph of an Arab male in his early 40s appeared on the projector screen. His thick beard was unkempt, and he looked disheveled and exhausted.

After clearing his throat, the lieutenant said, "This man is Sharif Jameel. He is the enemy combatant captured in last night's operation. Our records indicate he was a former schoolteacher turned Iraqi army. Shiite, not Sunni. Let go with the rest of them in '03."

"Whose dumbass decision was that?" somebody groused from the rear of the room.

"I have the floor," the officer said firmly before his expression cracked. "I believe his name was Paul. But there's no sense fighting over spilled milk. Our job is to mop it up."

"Mop them up," the same voice added.

"Potato, potahto," the lieutenant said. He allowed a few

chuckles to echo around the room, then cleared his throat to indicate that the time allotted for levity was over. "The good news is that Sharif is singing like a canary. Not just that, but he was sitting on nearly a ton of explosives, RPGs, ammo, and EFPs."

EFP stood for explosively formed penetrator, Trapp knew. They were a form of IED that had increasingly entered the insurgents' repertoire and had quickly become the single deadliest killer of US and Iraqi troops. An explosive detonation heated a piece of metal to temperatures of thousands of degrees before hurling it toward a target. The superheated metal cut through the armor plating on tanks, Bradleys, and MRAPs with pitiful ease before cooling and shattering into hundreds of jagged shards traveling nearly at the speed of sound once it was inside the vehicle's personnel compartment with predictably messy results.

Sikorski shot up his hand, waving it energetically until the lieutenant called on him. "What's the bad news, sir?"

"I can always rely on you to bring the mood down, huh, Private Sikorski?"

"It's what I do best, sir. That and—"

"Killing jihadis," the officer said with an audible roll of his eyes. "Yes, Sikorski. I've heard that one before. Say it too many more times and I'll put you in for a psych eval."

"I'll workshop some new material then, sir."

"That would be wise." The lieutenant coughed into his palm, then continued. "The bad news is that we also recovered a casing from a Misagh-1 MANPAD. For those of you who didn't pay attention in high school, that's an Iranian surface-to-air missile. A copy of a Chinese design, but a hell of a lot more potent than the 1970s junk that's been floating around in insurgent hands until now."

"Shit," Trapp muttered.

"Shit is right," the lieutenant agreed. "And that's why the

colonel is so interested in what you boys found last night. If more than a few of these missiles have made it across the border, then our air mobility is in grave danger. IEDs in the dirt and missiles in the air is a real bad combo."

He cleared his throat and turned to the next slide. "Evidence found at the site indicates that it was being run by the Sheibani Network. For anyone who wasn't paying attention the last five times we rolled up one of their facilities, they're quickly becoming the preeminent pain in our collective asses. Intelligence indicates that a third of all captured munitions in our area of responsibility come from this one Iranian-backed group, and that proportion is rising quickly."

Sikorski stuck up his hand once again. "Lieutenant?"

"What is it, Private?"

"I was hoping you had some more good news for me, sir."

"As a matter of fact, I do. Mr. Jameel was most cooperative when the full gravity of his present predicament was explained to him. He gave up two locations: another Sheibani Network safe house and a residential address. We intend to hit both of them tonight before they have a chance to disappear into the ether. Any questions at this point?"

"Do we have any information on expected numbers of defenders?" Breyer asked without looking up from a pad on which he was making copious notes.

"Working on it. Pattern of life analysis from previous overhead surveillance of the area indicates that the residential address is occupied by a family. We judge it likely that this is a secondary target."

"We'll take the safe house," the operator stated.

"No dice," Myers interjected. "The 75th sniffed out the lead on this one. Our guys get to hit the safe house. Same squad as last night for the sake of continuity. Policy is clear on this one."

The operator—though only an NCO—locked gaze with Captain Myers for a few seconds with the testosterone-flooded intensity of a rutting stag before dropping his eyes back to his pad and grunting, "Fine."

"We'll break here," the intel lieutenant interjected after a suitable pause to allow the tension to die down. "I want everyone back here in two hours. We'll draw up mission packs for both squads. Dismissed."

A general cry of "Hooah" rang out, accompanied by the scraping of chairs on the concrete floor.

"Sergeant Trapp," Myers said, lifting his head from his paperwork. "A word?"

Sikorski shot Trapp a mock-pitying look but couldn't conceal his grin as he turned to leave. Trapp winced back, then walked to the front of the briefing room and stood to attention in front of the officer.

"At ease," Myers said, dismissing the formality with a flick of his fingers. "Sergeant, you mind telling me exactly what the fuck you were thinking last night?"

Trapp judged that until he had more information, it was best to play things simple. "Sir?"

Myers narrowed his gaze. "Are we going to play this game?"

"I didn't think I was playing—"

"Where did you apprehend the suspect, Sergeant?"

"The basement of the target farmhouse, sir. It was in my after-action report."

"Exactly where in the basement, Trapp?"

"A—" Trapp paused as he realized where the captain was going with this. "An escape tunnel, sir."

"A tunnel," Myers repeated. "So let's circle back to my initial question. What the fuck were you doing going in there without backup? You know who has to write the letter to your family if you take a bullet to the face, Sergeant?"

"If it makes it easier for you, sir," Trapp said, "I don't have any."

"Common sense or family?" Myers asked acidly.

With a wry grin, Trapp replied, "Either."

Myers circled the finger in the air. "Well, the 75th is your family now, understood? And none of us want to see you under a white cross in Arlington. Least of all me. You're a good Ranger, Trapp. And you're a hell of a lot more useful to me alive than dead. Let's keep it that way."

3

"Did you hear?"

"Hear what, Sikorski?" Trapp asked, turning to see that the soldier had a sour look on his face.

"Those Delta assholes pulled rank. I guess they got word to the colonel, and he gave the okay for them to hit the safe house instead of us. We got shunted off to Special Teams, like usual," he said before disdainfully hiking up a mouthful of dip and spitting out the side of his mouth.

This wasn't the first time that Delta had muscled in on a Ranger operation. Trapp guessed it probably wouldn't be the last. It came with the territory of having a colonel from Delta in command of Task Force Center.

He was annoyed but didn't show it. Deliberately. A year back, before he made sergeant, he might've had a different reaction. But now he was a fire team leader with soldiers of his own to look out for. A few months from now, he might head up his own squad. Then again, his contract was nearly up. Maybe he'd quit the Army altogether. Sip mai tais on a beach somewhere and do something more rewarding with his life than hitching his wagon to a freight train of slaughter.

If he didn't get stop-lossed, that was.

"Sikorski, when did you find the time to have your ear surgically attached to the ground?" Trapp asked.

The joke provoked a grudging smile, as he'd suspected it might. Sikorski packed a fearsome temper into an ordinarily sunny demeanor, but his moods came and went like summer squalls.

He reached up and wiggled his left ear. "It's detachable, see? I just pull it off, and all the little birdies fly right to me."

"Well, it is what it is," Trapp said, repeating a refrain that might as well be surgically inked onto his own skin, given how often he found himself repeating it. "And hey, maybe this was the day you were supposed to die. Consider this your lucky escape. Divine intervention. Whatever you want to call it. We hit the secondary target instead. Who knows, maybe we'll turn up a diamond in the rough."

"COMM CHECK," Trapp shouted over the roar generated by a row of half a dozen Blackhawk helicopters parked side by side on the runway, their rotors spinning nearly at takeoff velocity. In turn, the soldiers in his fire team confirmed that their radios were working.

Each man was clear on the parameters and rules of engagement for their revised operation. Frustrating as each found the last-minute change of plans, it wasn't an unusual occurrence. Six years into the Global War on Terror, the halcyon days when operators were afforded weeks of preparation before hitting a target were long gone. Hell, at the relatively ancient age of just twenty-three years young, Trapp had never even gotten to experience them. The concept of operations for 21st century counterterrorism professionals emphasized speed above all else. Speed kept the enemy off balance. Speed kept fellow Americans alive. Speed led to dead terrorists, and there was no higher goal for Task Force Center than that.

Trapp shot the Blackhawk's crew chief a thumbs-up to signal that he and his men were ready to roll. As the moustachioed airman touched the tips of his thumb and index finger and turned away to relay that information to the pilots, he pulled his night vision aids into place and bathed the world in green. Around the chopper's confined cabin, he saw Sikorski and the others had done the exact same. It was difficult to make out expressions on their faces as they sat back, cradling their weapons. Were they excited?

Afraid?

It didn't matter. They would follow their orders.

Now all that was left to do was wait.

It didn't take long. Like the killers in the bellies of their birds, tonight's pilots and airmen were also members of the elite special operations community—the 160th Special Operations Aviation Regiment, otherwise known as the Night Stalkers. They too understood that the need for speed was paramount.

The choppers rose off LSS Anaconda's rubber-scarred asphalt one by one, spaced about five seconds apart. First came the three aircraft carrying the Delta team hitting the primary target. They angled sharply into the darkness, leaving a trail of burned aviation fuel behind them. Then it was the Rangers' turn.

Trapp's stomach dropped away as the chopper rose into the air. A radio transmission squawked into his earpiece, informing him that the regular Army unit tasked with creating a security screen five kilometers out from the target was moving into position. They would also provide the Quick Reaction Force, though he hoped that it wouldn't prove necessary.

"Fucking B-team shit," Sikorski grumbled through the fire team's radio net.

"Cut it out," Trapp said, raising his voice over the background roar of the Blackhawk's powerful engines. "Eyes on the prize until we're back in these choppers, you understand? And keep the radio clear unless you've got something important to say."

Sikorski gritted his teeth but reluctantly nodded his agreement. He sat back, his neck rigid with tension. Trapp didn't push it any further. He knew it was just the soldier's way of blowing off steam, of coming to terms with the fact that he was imminently, willingly placing himself in harm's way. He looked away and ran his fingers over his weapons and equipment, even though he'd already done so a dozen times. Each of the men in this helicopter was going through their own private ritual right now. Maybe this was his.

Powerful gusts of hot desert air flushed through the open sides of the helicopter as the minutes ticked by, tugging at Trapp's dark fatigues and momentarily cooling his sweat-beaded brow. It was a losing battle. A droplet of the salty liquid rolled haltingly down the side of his temple before the wind tugged it into his mouth. The taste was sharp and bitter. He fiddled with his rifle. Checked his ammunition was stowed in the same pouches it had been five minutes ago, and the five minutes before that.

"Five minutes out," the crew chief called out, holding out the same number of digits on his right hand to emphasize the message. "Get ready."

Trapp swallowed and stared out into the darkness of night. Occasionally they passed a small settlement in the distance, just a few glimmers of electric light on a blanket of sandy blackness. Sometimes there was the outline of a building against the ground which likely housed men and women and children who lived much as their grandparents had, and then it was gone.

"Sixty seconds."

"Buddy check," Trapp called out, turning to Muniz and checking that all the soldier's gear was where it was supposed to be. Anxiety flickered in his stomach, but he kept his tone steady. "You all know what you have to do. Don't take any unnecessary risks."

"What about tunnels, Sergeant?" someone replied over the radio. "Are we supposed to follow your lead, or..."

The soldier's train of thought reached neither a conclusion or an answer before the Blackhawk's nose dropped and the aircraft arrowed toward the ground. Though Trapp couldn't see them, he knew the other two choppers in the strike formation had followed suit. Somewhere beyond his field of view, an Apache helicopter gunship was also circling, its crew desperate to rain hell down on anyone either brave or foolhardy enough to shoot back.

Leaning out of the side of the helicopter, Trapp saw the target looming into sight. It was pitch black without a single glimmer of light—electric or otherwise. The building was rectangular, surrounded by a chest-high metal fence whose purpose he surmised was to keep farm animals in, not heavily armed operators out. Around it was arrayed several outbuildings, none of which was obviously occupied.

"Ten, nine..." The crew chief started counting down, his tone calm and unruffled as though he did this every night.

Trapp reflected that he probably did.

Right on time, the man hit "One."

A painful jolt ran up his spine as the Blackhawk's wheels met solid earth. Trapp didn't allow himself time to worry about it. He urged his soldiers out of the chopper—not that they needed any encouragement. Even to Trapp's cynical, perennially unsatisfied eye, they looked like a well-oiled machine.

"Go, go!"

Boots thudded against the rocky, sandy ground. Backwash from the rotors hurled dust and tiny stones into the air. They scoured every square inch of exposed skin, and he squeezed his eyes shut, temporarily blinding himself to avoid suffering a more permanent fate. On either flank of the bird that had just disgorged Trapp and his fire team, another Blackhawk was doing the same. He ignored them and sprinted ahead, knowing that each team had its own objective.

Sikorski reached the metal fence first and let his rifle fall to his chest as he reached out and vaulted it in one impressive leap. The second he was over, he dropped into a crouch, bringing the weapon back up to his shoulder to cover the rest of the team. Muniz came last, weighed down by the battering ram.

"Over," Trapp called, and Sikorski pushed out of his squat immediately and dashed for the building's only visible door, covering the source of danger the moment he stopped. Behind them, the first Blackhawk lifted back into the sky, followed an instant later by the next. The howl of their engines faded quickly, though partly it was the effect of the adrenaline blocking out everything that didn't present an immediate danger.

Trapp hurled himself against the farmhouse's brick wall hard enough to elicit an audible grunt, which was followed momentarily by two more thuds as the remaining members of the team joined him.

"Ram," Sikorski cried out as he pulled a concussion grenade off his plate carrier.

"Ready," Muniz replied.

"Hit it," Trapp said.

Almost before the second word escaped his mouth, the battering ram smashed into the door about two inches above where a lock would ordinarily be—but wasn't. The heavily muscled Ranger holding it had done this hundreds of times between training and the real thing. The best lock on the market would not have stood a chance.

The door in front of him certainly didn't. The top third of it simply shattered into chunks and splinters. Sikorski pulled the pin on the concussion grenade and tossed it through the hole the ram had created.

"Flash out," he called. From the other side of the building, Trapp heard a similar cry. He took a deep breath, shoved his fingers into his ears, and squeezed his eyes shut.

Three seconds later, right on cue, the grenade detonated.

In balletic synchrony, the four members of the fire team stepped over the now-discarded ram and into the farmhouse, with Sikorski on point. The beams of the laser aiming aids on their rifles resembled lightsabers as they panned across the otherwise empty space inside. As the young yet hellishly experienced soldier entered the room, sticking to the far right wall, Trapp did the same on the left. Their movements echoed the previous night, and the one before that, the basics hammered into them during week after week of practise in shoot-houses stateside and perfected after months of the real thing.

Trapp kept his back to the wall as he swept the aim of his rifle left and right across what was evidently the building's kitchen. Metal pans hung on hooks, and he was forced to step around a small gas stove stowed by the wall. Somewhere outside, a dog belatedly started howling a warning, the cry frantic and pained.

Too late, pooch.

His legs moved as if by muscle memory, as if they were fastened to tracks and could do only one thing. His pulse jackhammered in his temple. He felt his cone of vision narrowing —another familiar effect of the adrenaline. He forced himself to check left and right, down and up, dropping his rifle as another member of his team stepped into his line of fire, then raising it just as quickly.

"Clear," Sikorski called out.

"Clear," the other members of the team concurred.

"Next door," Trapp said, his voice tight. "Keep moving."

The fire team moved toward an internal doorway on the other side of the kitchen. Trapp stayed back to provide cover as they got ready to breach.

And then it started to open.

As though he was watching some low-budget Hollywood comedy, Trapp saw the other members of his team backpedal away from the entranceway, hurriedly bringing up their rifles as they prepared to face this new potential threat.

But they were too late.

A shape stepped through the door. All that Trapp could make out through his night vision was that the person was tall. And carrying a weapon.

He squeezed his trigger before Sikorski or any of the others even had their weapons halfway up. The rifle's discharge was impossibly loud in the confines of the cramped kitchen. His ears—already ringing from the concussion grenade—now screamed like banshees. The shape dropped to the ground, dead before it landed.

"Go," Trapp shouted, first to react. He ran toward the body and kicked the weapon aside, dropping to his knee for a moment to check the man's pulse.

Definitely gone.

It wasn't an act of compassion. Not really. He just needed to confirm that he wasn't leaving a threat in his rear.

As he momentarily paused, the rest of the fire team stepped into the unknown. Trapp rose and followed the green laser beam stretching out ahead of him. The faint scent of oils and spices gave way to a forgotten musk as he passed through the open doorway into a hallway. It wasn't long. On the right-hand side were two doors. The second one was half open. There was a sound coming from behind it, though it was indistinct.

"Keep moving," Trapp barked. "Sikorski, cover that second door."

"On it," came the terse reply.

The remaining members of the team moved as one. Trapp and Chambers covered the first doorway. Muniz held up two fingers then kicked the door in, revealing an empty bedroom. The bed itself was just a single mattress on the floor, covered in a couple of stained sheets. Next to it was an unloaded pistol and half a dozen rifle magazines, as well as a scattering of unspent rounds that crunched underfoot.

"Clear!"

Only a couple of seconds having elapsed since they breached the door, the three soldiers swung back around into the hallway.

"What the fuck?" a voice shouted.

"Gun!" another cried as the second doorway swung open and a man rushed out and away from the Rangers. A pistol was clutched in his right hand. He had something pressed against his chest with his left forearm. It looked like a bag, or—

No...

Trapp almost gagged as the shape in the tango's arms started to wriggle and kick, flashes of white and dark amid the green. A pained, scared cry rang out in the high-pitched voice of a young boy. Acid rose in his throat.

"Don't shoot!" he cried out loudly, an urgent stridency in his tone. "Piece of shit has a hostage. It's a kid."

"Copy," came the quick-fire reply.

"Keep pushing forward," Trapp shouted, revulsion now driving him on. What kind of man could use a child like that? Not one that deserved to survive the night.

The four men moved up the hallway as one. As they reached the doorway that the hostage-taker had just emerged from, it flew open a second time, bouncing back off the wall amid a shower of dust.

"Civilians!" Sikorski cried out in warning. A child ran

toward Trapp, followed by the pale green silhouette of a naked woman.

"What the hell?" Trapp muttered. He stared stupidly down at the kid sprinting surprisingly quickly in his direction. What was he supposed to do? Tackle it?

He'd never been good with kids.

The child was through his legs and out of the door behind before he had a chance to react. He grabbed the woman instead, letting his rifle fall against the clip on his chest and grabbing her by the torso before slamming her to the ground, soft flesh meeting hard earth. She cried out in terror, the Arabic words as unintelligible as they were crystal clear. The force of the impact caused him to wince, but he didn't have time to search her, and this was safest for everybody involved.

"What the hell is going on?" Sikorski asked, dropping to a knee and pinning the woman to the ground with an arm bar.

"Where's the kid?" Trapp replied, panting as he reached into a pouch for a set of flex-cuffs. He pulled them up and cinched them tight around the prisoner's wrists. She kept kicking, crying out, and jerking her chin down the hallway. "I'm guessing it's hers."

"Shit. They probably both are," Sikorski replied in grim realization. "That bastard."

Trapp tied the woman's ankles and rose back to his feet. "She's not going anywhere. Let's move."

A single gunshot rang out, muffled by the farmhouse's thick walls. Trapp glanced up as though he could see right through them. Before he had a chance to react, a fierce battle erupted outside. A smattering of different weapons loudly announced their presence—and not all of them matched those carried by his fellow Rangers. An occasional explosive thump punctuated the chaos.

"Sounds like he wasn't alone," Sikorski muttered.

"Yup," Trapp agreed. "Sounds like."

The most obvious explanation was that more militants had been hiding out in the farm's outbuildings. Judging by the volume of fire now ringing out, those elements were now engaging the rest of the assault team outside.

Suppressing the urge to simply sprint directly toward the danger, Trapp took stock of the situation. They had at least two civilian children to watch out for—the one that had been taken hostage, and the one he'd stupidly allowed to slip through his legs. Add one cold-blooded hostage-taker and an unknown number of armed insurgents, and things had the potential to slip rapidly from not great to really fucking bad—and quickly.

He quickly outlined a plan, finishing with, "Alive is better. But I'd rather the kid survived than this motherfucker, no matter how bad Command wants to get their claws into him. Understood?"

"Hooah!"

4

The radio net was exploding with the stressed, terse and yet relentlessly professional commentary of trained soldiers in combat as Trapp's team exited the farmhouse through a window to avoid exposing themselves to incoming fire.

"Friendlies coming out!"

The news that their target had taken a hostage had already been communicated. Worse still, he had somehow slipped through the net outside in the chaos that resulted from the other two Ranger fire teams coming under attack.

"Got one!" a soldier called out from a crouched firing position behind a rusted-out pickup truck that had long ago lost its wheels, briefly popping his head up to get eyes on his kill as he pumped his fist with satisfaction. A round sparked off the truck's chassis just inches from his freshly exposed head, causing him to duck and curse.

"Don't get cocky," another replied. "That one nearly split your dome clean open."

"Anyone see where he went?" Trapp called out. "My guys are free. We'll go after him."

"That way," a sergeant replied, jerking his hand out and pointing into the darkness. Overhead, the sound of rotors echoed out of the sky. "Toward the wadi. Fuck."

That final epithet was occasioned by a scatter of incoming rounds kicking up a shower of sand barely half a foot from where he was crouched. He rose up a few inches and unleashed half his magazine toward the outbuilding the insurgents had stationed themselves inside. They cracked harmlessly against the thick brick walls, sending clouds of dust shimmering down, but at least temporarily diminished the rate of incoming fire.

"Rogers, Brown," the sergeant shouted. "Give me covering fire on three. All you got."

He turned to Trapp. "Good luck. I hope you get them."

"Yeah, me too," he replied grimly, thinking of the terror that boy must currently be experiencing. It stirred a shadow of memory in him that he'd spent years attempting to forget.

"On me," he called to his own guys. "You know what to do."

"One," the sergeant called out loudly.

"Two."

On three, one of the other Rangers bounced up and tossed a grenade toward the outbuilding. A second later, another did the same. As soon as they hit the deck, the rest of the squad opened up with everything they had. The gunfire crackled at about the same time the pair of grenades detonated in quick succession, instantly—if briefly—silencing the incoming rounds.

"What the hell are you waiting for?" the first Ranger shouted. "A fucking embossed invitation? Go!"

Trapp didn't need telling twice. He sprinted into the darkness, his rifle pressed tight against his shoulder as his neck rotated like a well-oiled gimbal, scanning the ground underneath him for hazards, then left, ahead, right, down, left, and ahead and right. It never stopped. To stop was to miss something, and to miss something was to die.

Tiny stones scrabbled underneath his boots as they came into contact with the riverbed's unsteady surface. He skidded a few feet, then slowed his pace fractionally to compensate. The dust in the air coated his mouth and tongue, growing thicker with every strained breath.

"I see him!" Sikorski said. "About 50 yards."

"I'll take your word for it," Trapp replied, trusting the man's superior eyesight—and his depth perception, which was notoriously difficult through the night vision goggles they both wore. "He still got the kid with him?"

"How the hell should I know?" Sikorski shot back. "Big Green don't pay me enough to moonlight as the fucking Hubble Telescope. The day I get that sweet NASA money is the day you get your answer."

Trapp laughed despite—or perhaps because of—the peril of the situation. His boots drummed a steady beat against the stony ground. He kept his finger off the trigger just in case he slipped and fell and pulled it accidentally. He couldn't have a kid's death on his conscience.

"Forty yards," Sikorski said, his voice already all business. "We're gaining on him."

That had to mean that the fleeing militant still had his hostage, Trapp realized. He was weighed down by the child whose life he had mortgaged in order to pay for his own.

Bastard, Trapp thought grimly, vowing to do whatever it took to ensure the trade fell through.

Now an indistinct shape appeared through his goggles. He had no idea how the hell Sikorski had managed to spot their target almost thirty seconds earlier.

"There's something up ahead," Sikorski called, his voice equally hoarse from the thick clouds of dust they were sucking up as they ran and backed by the panting from the rest of the fire team—Trapp included. Running with a weapon, a vest stuffed with armored plates, and a full load-out of gear wasn't easy. But then, neither was carrying a struggling child.

"Can you be any less specific?" Trapp replied in an acerbic, strained tone.

"Doing my best here, Sergeant."

The sound of the battle behind them wasn't fading. If anything, it was growing more intense. Trapp radioed the helicopters circling menacingly in the sky above and requested a pair of eyes in the sky, only to be informed that they had been ordered to buzz the farm in a show of intent.

"We're on our own," he informed the fireteam.

"Ain't that always the way," Sikorski laughed before his tone turned deadly serious. "Hit the deck!"

All three of them complied without asking why. They'd served together long enough to know that sometimes it was better to do, not die. Trapp threw himself down, skidding on his chest along the rocky ground. His gloves bore the brunt of the impact, but a stone dragged his helmet chinstrap away and scraped the underside of his chin hard enough to draw blood.

"Fuck!" he cried out before forgetting all about it as three rapid muzzle flashes sparked out of the darkness ahead, amplified by his night vision gear. They were followed a second later by the cracks of gunfire as the sound caught up.

Trapp leveled his weapon, knowing he needed to press the pursuit now and not allow the militant to pin them down. Speed was paramount. "Okay, warning shots. Let's give him something to think about."

"About time," Sikorski said. He was crouched behind a low boulder that wasn't nearly large enough to cover his bulky frame. He rolled onto his back, freed his rifle, then bounced up and fired half a dozen shots into the sky. There was nothing behind in that direction but empty desert for dozens of miles, save perhaps an extremely unlucky camel.

"Move in pairs," Trapp said. "Sikorski, with me."

They leapfrogged forward, the two men scampering forward as low as possible as the other two cracked warning shots into the sky. Occasionally their prey replied, but his fire was wayward and hurried.

Both groups had slowed, but Trapp's fireteam—with one pair always on the move—steadily gained on their target.

"Shit," Sikorski swore.

"What?"

"That's a fucking pickup truck," he replied. Trapp crouched on one knee, fired three shots into the dark, then squinted at the shape that Sikorski had mentioned earlier. To him, it was still an indistinct blob of green. Maybe there was a shape, but...

"You sure?"

"Yup."

"Leroy One Nine," Trapp radioed immediately, using the callsign of the bird that had carried them for tonight's mission. "Our prey is preparing to go mobile. I'm going to need eyes overhead stat. Over."

"Copy your last," came an unhurried reply. "Location?"

Trapp panted as he directed the helicopter toward their position without letting off the chase. "Target has a hostage. A child. Say again, target has a noncombatant minor with him. Do not engage. Just make sure you don't lose him. Is the QRF en route?"

"Affirmative," the special operations aviator transmitted. "And understood. Moving to you now. Leroy One Nine out."

The clatter of rotors subtly changed over the farm, growing first marginally quieter, then much, much louder as one of the scarcely visible birds swooped toward them. It took a matter of seconds, and as lactic acid tore at the muscle fibres in his legs, Trapp envied the machine's easy, powerful grace. He forced himself onward.

They were now only twenty yards away from their target. This close, even Trapp could make out that the shape ahead really was a pickup truck—covered by what he guessed was camouflage netting or maybe just a dusty tarp. That would probably have been enough to hide it from the aerial surveillance. That was the downside of these rush jobs. Even with the best of intentions, corners got cut.

The hostage taker was attempting to drag it off while maintaining his grip on the kid. As Trapp watched, he threw the child powerfully to the ground at his feet, crouched behind him, and fired the best part of his pistol's magazine toward his pursuers without letting up. The second he was done, he grabbed the child, placed the muzzle of his weapon against the kid's temple and dragged him behind the bed of the pickup and out of sight, shouting something loudly in Arabic.

"Anyone catch that?" Sikorski called over the roar of Blackhawk's rotors.

"My Hajji is a little rusty," Chambers quipped as he skidded to a halt. "But I'm guessing he's telling us to back the fuck up or he'll shoot."

"You watch too many B movies," Trapp said, taking a knee —and a couple of deep breaths. "But you're probably right. Okay, we need to flank him. Sikorski, you think you can put a couple rounds in the engine block without hitting the kid?"

"You bet."

"Then you and me that way," Trapp said, pointing to the left-hand side of the truck. "And don't miss."

The fireteam split into two pairs without another word needing to be spoken. As they did, the camo netting came completely free of the pickup, and the sound of a door opening then slamming shut was just barely audible over the roar of the chopper.

The truck's brake lights flashed as the engine coughed into life, ejecting thick smoke into the air in the process.

"Nearest town's three clicks to the northeast," Leroy One

Nine's pilot radioed. "If he makes it there, he's gone. Place is like a fucking rabbit warren."

"Tell me something I don't know," Trapp muttered without transmitting as he sprinted toward the truck's bed.

The engine roared a second time, and its wheels kicked a shower of rocks and sand toward him. Sikorski was a couple of paces ahead, but as they closed within five or ten feet, the pickup began building speed. For another couple seconds, they managed to keep pace, trepidation and worry knotting Trapp's stomach as he recognized what was about to happen.

"No shot," Sikorski yelled as the truck peeled away. "Shit!"

"I'm on him," the chopper transmitted. "You guys need a lift?"

"Stay with him," Trapp replied, his lungs straining with the effort to speak.

He kept running, his rifle banging against his chest, swinging from side to side from its clip. The pickup slowed to negotiate an obstacle—some kind of boulder—in the path ahead. Trapp used the time this bought and urged his straining body to give him one last jolt of strength as he sprinted through a noxious cloud of smoke, dust, and grit.

His vision narrowed to a slit, his breath constricted in his chest and throat as he raced forward, head down and arms pumping by his side. Out of the corner of his eye, he saw Sikorski disappearing behind him as he desperately tried to keep up.

The pickup's brake lights flashed red, and it came to a skidding stop before backing up a few feet. It was the break Trapp had been hoping for. He thrust off his right foot and flew through the air, colliding with the back of the truck and only barely hanging on as its driver finally worked his way around the obstacle that had forced him to stop.

The vehicle lurched forward once again, the sudden motion causing Trapp to topple back. His gloved fingers slipped, the left-hand falling away entirely and sending an agonizing blast of pain through his right shoulder as that arm now took all his weight. He fell downward, his night vision goggles bashing against the rear of the truck and tearing clean off his helmet. Tears stung at his eyes—not just from the dust the vehicle's rear tires were kicking up but also the thought of how he was going to explain this to the unit's supply specialist without eating the check.

The toes of Trapp's boots skidded against the hard-packed riverbed as he clung, one-handed, desperately struggling to right himself as—worryingly—the pickup again began gaining speed.

"Leave it, Trapp!" he heard Sikorski cry out behind him, way behind now. "Let the chopper handle it."

And then his friend's voice was gone. His entire world was the throb of the helicopter's rotors, the roar of the truck's engine, and the clouds of dust and stone that blocked out what was left of his vision in the dark. With a monumental force of effort, he flung his left hand up and high, where it bounced off the back of the truck's bed and somehow—miraculously— held. The pressure on his right shoulder diminished but didn't disappear.

With this second point of leverage, Trapp pulled himself up and into the pickup's bed. It was empty, save a scattering of tools that made for a hard and unpleasant landing.

"Fuck!" he cursed as he fell, heavily, on his chest. The tools rattled underneath him, and he jolted painfully every time the truck's wheels hit a pothole. Which was frequently.

Lactic acid burned his calves and thighs, as well as almost every other muscle in his body. He forced it out of his mind, pushing himself up and reaching for the pistol thrust through a strap on his plate carrier. It wasn't exactly SOP to store it there, but everybody did it. And now Trapp was glad he had.

Two gunshots rang out in quick succession, splintering the

pickup's rear window before whistling off into the night. Trapp brought the pistol up and chambered a round, now cursing the loss of his low light optics.

All he could see through the cracked glass was a maelstrom of shapes in the darkness. He dared not risk opening fire, not without having clear sight of a target. Not with a kid inside the cabin.

Another gunshot. Nearer this time, though still at least a foot from where Trapp was crouched, hanging on to the bucking truck's bed for dear life as the cursed ride struggled to eject him. One by one, the tools and construction supplies surrounding him bounced up and flew out into the darkness.

Trapp knew he couldn't let this play out much longer. He knew his target was firing blind, probably over his shoulder as he battled with the steering wheel. But the asshole only had to get lucky once.

"Jason, what the hell you doing?" Sikorski's voice crackled through his ear. "I said let the chopper handle it."

"Hell no," Trapp murmured as he came to a decision. He reversed the pistol in his hand and used the grip to smash through the pickup's rear window, trusting his Kevlar-reinforced gloves to protect his hands. He swept left and right, clearing a hole big enough to fit his oversized frame through. It was going to be tight, especially when he factored in the thirty pounds of gear he was carrying.

Another flash briefly lit the pickup's cabin before fading to black. There was no glass left for the bullet to shatter. But even through the wind whipping through his helmet and the clamor of the helicopter overhead, there was no disguising how close that shot had come. He waited for another hammer blow to fall, but none came. Hope flared that the guy's weapon had run dry.

Better not wait to find out.

He switched the weapon in his hand once more and thrust

himself through the window. What was left of the glass tore at his fatigues and crunched underneath his boots as he scrambled for purchase.

As he was clambering into the truck, his enemy changed the rules of the game. The man behind the wheel stamped hard on the brakes, instantly taking the pickup from at least seventy miles an hour to an almost dead stop in the blink of an eye. Clouds of dust billowed outside, coating all the windows. The last thought that went through Trapp's mind before inertia flung him forward was, *Ah, shit.*

In the chaos as he flew through the pickup's cramped cabin, he lost his grip on the pistol. He didn't have time to worry about what had happened to it before his right shoulder took a second powerful blow and he came to a rapid and unscheduled stop, slamming against the back of the driver's seat and snapping the mechanism inside from the force.

The seat folded shut, slamming the driver against the horn and letting out a single, mournful tone before it died.

Trapp groaned, all oxygen driven from his lungs from the impact. "Dammit."

Unable to breathe, barely able even to see, he knew he still had to act. Fast, while his enemy was sufficiently unbalanced for it to count.

Where's the kid?

Realizing his legs were still half-hanging out of the truck's rear window, Trapp jackknifed his knees toward his chest and brought them inside, then pushed himself backward against the truck's passenger seats, which were now covered in splintered glass.

"We're closing on you," Sikorski transmitted.

That was right. The truck was stopped. The longer he could keep this asshole here, the more the odds would change in his favor. Trapp patted his body for a weapon and realized almost absentmindedly that his rifle was still clipped to his chest. He reached for it and brought it up as quickly as he could.

But not fast enough.

"Stop!" the driver yelled in thickly accented English.

Trapp froze, the rifle only halfway up. His target had reacted quicker, perhaps because the boy was still clutched to his breast. And the man's pistol was pressed against the kid's right temple, hard enough to wrench his neck almost to his shoulder.

"Drop the weapon," Trapp said with surprising calm, given the chaos he was surrounded by. Right now, he had possession of approximately none of the cards, and if his enemy was in his right mind, he probably knew that. So all he could do was bluff.

The reply came in quick, angered Arabic. Trapp didn't understand the words, but the meaning was plain.

Drop your gun or the kid gets it.

The boy's terrified dark brown eyes stared at him. He was trembling, too scared to speak. As Trapp's own eyes adjusted to the darkness, he saw tears seeping down the kid's face.

"Sixty seconds," Sikorski said, his voice tight from the effort of talking as he ran. "You couldn't have stopped him sooner?"

Trapp knew he didn't have that long. If this dragged on, either he would end up dead, or the boy, or both. At least, if the pistol's magazine had any bullets remaining.

"There's no way out of this," he said in that same measured tone. "You must know—"

He didn't have time to finish. In a flash the driver brought the muzzle of the pistol away from the kid's temple. Trapp reacted fast, knowing he wasn't close enough to grab the weapon, and made himself as small as possible—far from an easy task.

The gunshot was impossibly loud in the truck's cramped cabin. It blew out the pickup's front passenger window.

Not dry, then.

Instantly Trapp realized what that was: the only warning he was going to get. He was too far away from the boy to grab him, and anyway the pistol was once more pressed against the child's skull. His own rifle was far too unwieldy to aim and fire quickly enough to affect the situation. Trying to reach for it would only risk the boy's life.

And he was clearly dealing with a sociopath.

"Okay," he muttered, staring blackly at the driver's shadowed face and committing it as best as possible to memory. The Blackhawk's engines thrummed overhead, its rotors creating a hurricane of downwash. "You win. I'll let you go."

He let his rifle fall against his chest as Sikorski reported, "Thirty seconds."

It was too long. This asshole was a couple seconds away from slotting the kid. Trapp levered himself backward, reaching for the passenger door handle with his left hand, not taking his eyes off the driver once.

Only as the door swung open did he switch his gaze to the child. He didn't know why he said it, but as he fell toward the ground and the driver stamped on the gas pedal to accelerate his fall, he whispered, "I'll come back for you."

5

The US Army doctor finished affixing the final bandage around Trapp's scraped and bruised arms. He was a man in his late 30s with the rank of captain and was paying an uncomfortable amount of attention to his wounds. Trapp just wanted a hot shower and to be able to lie down.

"I'm fine, sir, really. I'm sure you have something better to do."

The doc coughed into his hand, perhaps to conceal his amusement. "As a matter of fact, soldier, I don't. There's one of me for two hundred of you guys, and this is still the most interesting thing I've done all week."

"That's a good thing, I guess?" Trapp remarked as the doc tore open a sealed pack of antiseptic wipes and dabbed away a few spots of dried blood from his skin.

"You're probably right," the captain conceded. "At least if I was stationed back home, I'd get to deal with a few cases of venereal disease a week. But out here, there's nothing to fuck but camels and sand. Excuse my French."

"Yes, sir."

The doc sounded almost wistful as he continued. "It's hard to keep your skills sharp when anything serious gets medevacked straight to Germany. And you Special Forces types usually don't come and see me until your arm's hanging off your elbow by a thread."

"No, sir," Trapp said, keeping his responses simple and diplomatic.

"But don't go getting yourself shot on my account," the captain finished, tossing the trash into a yellow medical waste container. "It's not like I'd get to patch you up anyway."

"I'll bear that in mind." Trapp grinned.

"That's it," the doc said, collapsing onto a wheeled metal stool and rolling himself along the linoleum floor toward a computer stationed on an austere, sterile metal desk. "You should take it easy the next few days. That shoulder took a hell of a wrench. I'm guessing it'll be black and blue when you wake up in the morning. It's already got more color than I'd like."

He opened a nearby drawer and tossed over a few blister packs of over-the-counter painkillers and anti-inflammatories. "Take these—no more than two tablets three times a day. And I mean that. A stomach ulcer will keep you out of action much longer than that shoulder when it pops."

"I don't like painkillers," Trapp replied.

"Take them anyway. The anti-inflammatories at least. They'll help."

A sharp rap at the door drew Trapp's attention. Sikorski popped his head through. "Morning, Captain," he said. "I just thought I'd check in on your patient."

"He's free to go," the doc said, turning to his computer and starting to update Trapp's medical records. "Try to look after him a bit better, will you, Private?"

"I'll do my best, sir, but that's a bit above my pay grade."

The doc made a noncommittal grunt that sounded a little like one of despair and began tapping away at his keyboard.

Trapp took it as his cue to leave. He offered his thanks, zipped up his undershirt, and walked over to Sikorski.

"I'm a big boy, you know," he said, gesturing with his bandaged forearm. "And it's just a graze. I wouldn't even be here if the lieutenant hadn't ordered me to get patched up."

"Me too," Sikorski laughed before his expression turned serious. "But that's not why I'm here. I thought you'd want to know they started questioning that woman we picked up."

"Already?" Trapp replied, exhaustion tugging at his bones.

It was almost six a.m., and he was exhausted, both physically and emotionally. Every time he closed his eyes, he saw that kid staring back at him, face shadowed, eyes glistening with terror. How the hell must his mother feel, dragged out of her bed stark naked at three a.m. to the sound of gunfire, only to be hauled alone into the back of the chopper and carried off to an American base?

Sikorski flicked his fingers dismissively, though Trapp suspected he was concealing his true feelings on the matter. "You know what the interrogators say. The longer you let 'em sit, the wilder the story they'll try to sell you."

"But she's a noncombatant."

"Maybe. But she was in bed with the guy who shot at us and stole the kid."

"Stole *her* kid," Trapp corrected. "And don't you dare say potato/potahto."

"Wouldn't dream of it."

"Who's conducting the interrogation?" Trapp said, turning in the direction of the barracks. His fatigues were coated in dust, sand, and dirt and had the sticky feeling of clothes that had been worn far too long.

"You're not going to like it," Sikorski said, falling in alongside.

Trapp stopped dead. "Not Hook?"

"One and the same."

"I thought he was supposed to be heading back home."

"Guess not."

Trapp slapped his thigh, the sudden discomfort making him feel considerably more alert. He reversed his direction and walked in long, purposeful strides, leaving Sikorski in the dust.

"Where the hell are you going?"

"To watch," Trapp replied, his voice gruff. "You heard the captain."

"That's a first," Sikorski replied, breaking into a jog in order to catch up. Trapp realized that his friend had had time to shower and change while he'd been in the infirmary.

"Yeah, well, Pete Hook is a piece of shit."

For some reason, the thought of Hook alone in an interrogation room with a vulnerable woman made his skin crawl. The man was a civilian interrogator, contracted to SOCOM to fill an urgent operational need—and in the process bypassing whole swathes of checks and balances. He dressed like an operator, down to the thick beard and wraparound Oakley shades, despite the fact that he'd never once left the wire. More pertinently, he apparently hadn't heard that it was easier to catch flies with honey than vinegar.

"No argument here. But just to confirm, all you're planning on doing is *watching*, right?" Sikorski said, now jogging at Trapp's side in order to keep up. "Because I'm getting mixed messages."

"Sikorski, shut up."

"Just looking out for you, man" came a slightly affronted reply.

The interrogation compound was adjacent to the area set aside for Task Force Center and surrounded by an identical set of soaring concrete ramparts. Inside were more than two dozen identical interrogation rooms and holding cells for almost a hundred prisoners, as well as thousands of square feet of office space to house the analysts who tried to make sense of the untold hours of interrogation tape this place produced every single day and night.

In truth, it was the beating heart of the Special Operations task force. Without it, the whole organization would jolt to a shuddering halt. Signals intelligence was useful, but the insurgents had long since learned not to communicate through unencrypted radios and cell phones. Where they did, they'd adopted coded messages whose meaning was difficult to parse.

They would still have the physical intelligence squads like Trapp's collected every night, but without the crucial context that the prisoner interrogations provided, it would either mean nothing or take too long to prove actionable. And before long, the relentless special operations machine that was turning the tide of the insurgency in America's favor would grind to a halt.

Trapp barged into the interrogation center practically shouting at the first soldier he saw, "Where is she?"

Wordlessly, a terrified-looking young specialist pointed down a hallway. It was color-coded blue to distinguish it from the other interrogation wings, which had been decorated all in primary colors, as if out of a toddler's paint set. The harsh white overhead lights did nothing to improve Trapp's mood.

Every thirty feet or so along the hallway walls, two doors stood side by side. The left led into an observation room equipped with television monitors where analysts transcribed records of the interrogations and had a direct line to the task force's operations center in case anything time-sensitive was learned. The right led into the interrogation room, a fact which Trapp knew from long experience but could be deduced by noticing the presence of a colored lamp above the door.

Currently, the first interrogation room was occupied. The lamp flashed red.

Trapp almost entered it but held himself back at the last moment and turned the handle for the observation room instead. He pretended he didn't hear Sikorski breathing a sigh of relief behind him. An analyst looked up as he entered, eyes widening as he took in Trapp's filthy, dust-coated uniform.

"I'm just here to watch," Trapp muttered.

"What he said," Sikorski panted, closing the door behind him. "Just pretend we're not here."

The analyst nodded and turned his attention back to the transparent mirror on the wall in front of him. To his left-hand side was a computer monitor displaying a video feed of the interrogation that was irritatingly about half a second out of sync. An analog light panel on the desk indicated that the recording equipment was active, and an Arabic voice was being piped through the speaker on the walls. The female voice sounded stressed and exhausted.

But that wasn't what occupied Trapp's attention.

"Fuck," Sikorski muttered. "They could have at least given her something to wear."

Clenching his fists, Trapp emitted a guttural grunt. The woman was wrapped in a thick, faded red blanket decorated with a local design. It looked like someone had taken it from the farmhouse and given it to her to cover herself. She clutched it tightly to her chest with hands that were manacled to the desk, forcing her to hunch forward in order to protect her modesty. Her dark hair was limp and had formed into rattails which were draped across her left cheek.

"I told you already, I know nothing," the translator—also in the interrogation room—said. He was standing by the wall, his face impassive, though there was something about his posture that told Trapp he didn't like what he saw. "Where is my son? What have you done with my son?"

Hook stood at the woman's side, close enough that if she'd looked up at him, she would have had to crane her neck. He was wearing a tan T-shirt and had stuck one hand underneath it before crossing his arms, lifting the material so that half his belly was on show.

It was a disrespectful stance, especially for a woman who likely hadn't been in a room with another man unchaperoned since she was a young girl. Trapp could hardly imagine a worse way of building rapport. He understood the theory behind Hook's strategy of attempting to push the woman off balance; he just didn't agree with it. In his view they already had an easy in—her son was missing, taken by a psychopath.

What mother couldn't be convinced to save her own child?

"We have your boy. And you'll never see him again unless you tell me what I want to know."

After the interpreter translated Hook's statement, the prisoner wailed with despair. Trapp blinked, and the kidnapped boy's dark brown eyes flashed across his vision, as though the child was calling out for help from the beyond.

"You can't do this," the translator said over the sound of the woman's handcuff chain rattling against the metal desk. "I won't tell you anything until you bring me my son."

He flashed a loaded glance in Hook's direction, but the interrogator brushed him off, saying, "You're here to translate, that's all. Tell her I want to know the name of the man she was fucking. Tell her she was sleeping with a terrorist. In my book, that makes her an accomplice. We'll get our Iraqi friends to hang her in front of her kid. That should get her attention."

"That useless fuck," Trapp breathed, drawing a startled glance from the analyst sitting in front of them.

As the translator communicated his instructions, signaling his severe displeasure with his bristling posture as he spoke, the prisoner started to tremble. Trapp suspected that the reaction had little to do with the fact that the AC in the interrogation room was cranked all the way up. Fat, terrified tears dripped down her cheeks, staining the blanket and pooling on the metal table in front of her.

"Cry all you want," Hook said. "I'm not falling for your crocodile tears. And the longer you hold out on me, the worse I'll make it for you. You understand?"

The woman only shivered violently in response. It looked like she was going into shock—as though Hook's threats had pushed her over a psychological tipping point. Trapp felt sick watching. It was also unnecessary—and counterproductive. She was shutting down, not opening up. How could the interrogator not see it? He was too consumed by the caricature he'd constructed of what this woman was to see what was right in front of his nose.

Trapp frowned as he noticed Hook coiling his frame, wondering what the man was up to. His question was answered a second later as he watched the interrogator slam his open palm down on the table. The shock of the sudden explosion of aggression caused the prisoner to jerk back, the motion tugging the blanket out of her fingers and causing it to fall open around her breasts.

The chain snapped taut, and she was stopped dead by her handcuffs, her eyes wide, dark and terrified as she stared up at the interrogator.

It was a look Trapp knew well. One he'd hoped he would never see again. Perhaps an unrealistic aspiration in this line of work, but at least an honorable one.

"Fuck it," he said, spinning around on the toe of his boot and reaching for the door.

"Jason..." Sikorski murmured in a singsong, warning tone. "What are you thinking?"

"I'm not."

Out of the corner of his eye, Trapp saw that his friend was caught between two minds—whether to go after him or...

Something else.

As the door swung closed behind him, Trapp heard Sikorski hurriedly instruct the analyst to kill the camera feed. He didn't stop to consider whether his course of action was a wise one as he passed under the baleful gaze of a security camera before turning the exterior-latching handle of the door that led into the interrogation room.

Both Hook and the interpreter looked up in surprise as he entered, the door bouncing off the wall at his side.

"Sergeant," Hook began, "what the fuck do you think you're doing interrupting my interrogation?"

Trapp gritted his teeth. He felt the familiar sensation of rage building inside him. It was an emotion he'd learned to control in recent years but one he was always riding the edge of. "Get out."

Hook frowned, clearly not having expected that response. "What?"

Trapp jerked his thumb back into the hallway. "I said out. Quickly."

"Sergeant... Trapp," Hook said, disrespectfully squinting at the name patch even though he knew who he was talking to full well. "Unless you want to spend the next month in the stockade, I suggest you turn around and get the hell out of here. I'll be speaking to your CO no matter what you decide, but if you're smart, you'll make this easier on yourself."

It was the smug self-satisfaction etched into Hook's face that finally made Trapp snap. He launched himself into the interrogation room, not stopping until he had his fingers wrapped around the now cringing man's lapels. He dragged him up, easily lifting his weight so that he was forced to stand on tiptoes.

"Do we have a problem?" Trapp hissed. He didn't like inflicting physical violence, though he was called to do so increasingly frequently in his line of work. But he knew that he had an imposing presence.

And sometimes you needed to let your reputation do the talking.

"Are you insane?" Hook said, his voice strangled and reedy. "They'll court-martial you for this. Get your hands off me!"

"Do I look like I give a fuck?" Trapp asked, lowering his voice further and kind of liking the look of increasing concern in Hook's eyes. "This is how things are going to go. You're going to get the fuck out of this interrogation room. I don't care where you go as long as I don't see you again. And if I ever see you treating a woman—hell, any prisoner—like this again, you better know it'll be the last thing you do."

6

"I'm sorry you had to see that," Trapp said, turning away from the door to the interrogation room. The sound of scuffling behind it was still just audible as Sikorski dragged Hook away but grew fainter the farther into the room he walked.

His heart sank when he saw the prisoner. She had brought her legs up into her blanket and was hunched into a ball against her chair, leaning as far away from him as physically possible given the restraints that still chained her to the table.

"Dammit," he whispered. If Hook had been purposely trying to break this woman's desire to cooperate, he couldn't have done a better job of it. He caught the attention of the startled-looking translator and gestured at him to continue.

Trapp raised his palms apologetically as the soft sound of Arabic finally filled the harsh interrogation space. He concealed his distaste at the realization that his words were being mediated through the same voice as Hook's had been. It didn't seem like the right way to build rapport, but he didn't have any other choice. He'd stomped on a termite's nest by throwing the interrogator out, and it wouldn't take long before the consequences of that action marched back to bite him in the ass. He certainly didn't have long enough to find a new translator.

"That man doesn't represent all of us, okay?" he continued, inching toward the interrogation table with his palms still facing her. He consciously forced himself to relax his posture and to display every possible sign that he was friendly and unthreatening. The prisoner's gaze followed his every step without blinking once. Her eyes were dark and fearful.

He stopped a couple of feet from the metal table and— unthinkingly—reached into his pocket. The woman flinched. Trapp gritted his teeth, cursing his thoughtlessness, and slowly pulled out the keychain that he'd lifted from Hook's belt. He held it in front of her.

"If it's okay with you, I want to come closer so I can unlock those handcuffs," he said in a soft, soothing voice. He matched her gaze without staring, projecting as harmless an expression as he could. "They don't look comfortable."

Even after his words were translated, the prisoner didn't react. Trapp knew better than to continue his approach. She had to be in shock. Despite knowing that he was on the clock, he couldn't rush this. He left a few seconds after the inter- preter's voice faded away, the only sound that of the air condi- tioning fan humming gently in the background.

"I'm going to put the keys down on the table, okay?" he said. "I'll slide them over to you. It's the small one. You can't miss it."

He waited until the translator was done, then bent to set the keys down. He froze as the woman finally spoke.

"She says you can do it yourself," the translator said.

Trapp concealed the flush of exultation that fired within him at the sound of her voice. He was no expert at interroga- tion, but certain basic principles stood to reason: You couldn't get anywhere if your subject didn't speak. Conversation was the foundation that rapport was built upon.

He had his opening.

"Thank you," he said.

He moved slowly and gently toward her, taking everything in stages, making sure that his hands were always visible as he approached her and entered the key into the lock. A little click later and the first manacle was open. One more and the prisoner yanked her hands toward her, massaging her wrists.

Trapp allowed her all the time she needed. He backed away a few steps as he planned what to do next. He burned to ask her about the man who had taken her son as a hostage but knew he couldn't rush this. Several times, her eyes flicked up to look at him. He waited to see if she would speak first.

Finally she did so, her words mediated through the interrogator's even tone. Her own was surprisingly powerful, despite her current predicament. "Does that man work for you?"

"No," he replied, shaking his head vehemently. "If anything, it's the other way around. He outranks me."

"But you attacked him."

Trapp inclined his head. "I did."

"Why?"

Frowning, he tried to put words to the feeling he'd experienced when he saw the way Hook was acting. "I don't like it when men treat women that way. I apologize for the way he acted."

Trapp gestured at the empty chair, aware of the power dynamic that existed between them as he towered over her. "Would it be okay with you if I sat down?"

She took a few seconds to consider the request, finally acceding with a quick nod of her head.

"Thank you," he said, lifting the chair and swinging it around the table so that it sat next to her, not opposite. He grinned. "My neck was starting to hurt looking down at you."

"Where is my son?" she asked, the translator's tone not

quite matching the intensity of the way the words spilled out of her mouth.

For a moment, Trapp thought she meant the child whose kidnapping he'd failed to stop. Only belatedly did he realize that another child had been present in the building that night. The militant had only taken one hostage, not two. And since no adults had been left at the compound, that meant the child must have been taken back to camp with the returning Rangers.

"Safe," he assured her. "We don't treat children badly here. I'm sure someone's feeding him as we speak."

Still huddled in a ball, the woman said, "I need to see him."

Trapp turned and stared directly into the video camera on the wall. "Then I'll make that happen."

"Thank you."

"It's the right thing to do." Trapp shrugged. "He's your kid. Can I ask your name?"

"Nadia."

"That's a lovely name. I'm Jason."

Nadia didn't respond to this particular piece of information, though Trapp thought he sensed a minute softening in her rigid posture. She shifted in the chair and hugged her legs. Conscious that his time was running before somebody—hopefully not an MP—dragged him out of here like he'd done to Hook, he realized he had to press on.

"You have another son, right?"

Nadia tensed up. She didn't say anything.

"I tried to stop the man who took him, but"—he gestured at the cuts and the shadows of bruises on the skin of his arms and face—"I wasn't fast enough. I'm sorry."

Tears formed in the corners of Nadia's eyes. Guilt wracked Trapp at the realization that he was using her love for her son as leverage. He reassured himself that it was in a good cause, but it left a nasty taste in his mouth. Was this really any more honorable than Hook's approach? It didn't feel that way.

"What happened?" Nadia choked.

He concentrated on the emotion in her voice, not the cool detachment in the translator's. He didn't answer directly.

"The man who took your son, who was he?"

Instead of answering, Nadia clammed up. She dropped her forehead to her knees and started to shake. Though he couldn't see them, it was evident that tears were streaming down her face.

Trapp opened his mouth to reassure her but cut himself off. He sensed that anything he might conjure up would be for himself, not her. He itched to embrace the woman but worried that that too was a selfish gesture, especially given the cultural differences around men and women interacting over here. He'd never felt more impotent. This was a battlefield on which neither the Army nor anything in his life so far had trained him to fight.

"Please, Nadia," he implored. "I can't do anything if you don't help me."

"He is my husband," Nadia said, the words punching through walls of barely broken sobs.

"But he threatened your son," Trapp said, keeping his tone even and non-judgmental.

"Omar is not a good man," she said. "He—"

She cut herself off before going any further and rocked back and forth on the chair, still clutching her knees. Out of sight, Trapp dug his fingernails into his thigh, trying but failing to create a relief valve for the frustration building inside him. There was something about the way she described her own husband that was horribly reminiscent of his own past. Demons that he'd long since squashed now reared their heads.

"He *what*, Nadia? Talk to me, okay? Tell me about him. We can work out how to fix this."

But she wouldn't stop crying. Every few seconds she looked up, her eyes darting around the harshly lit interrogation room as if searching for her son before fresh tears cast loose.

Trapp traded glances with the translator, whose expression gave away nothing. He knew he had to change tack. He had a few minutes left, maybe even less than that, before someone further up the command chain dragged him out of this room and had him cleaning toilets for a month—if he was lucky. Hook would be raising hell out there. The man had an ego the size of a Texas steer. It wouldn't be able to take the prick that Trapp had given him.

"Can I tell you something personal?" he said. "It's something I haven't told anyone in a very long time."

The translator's eyes flickered toward him before quickly looking away. Trapp gestured at the man to continue.

Nadia didn't respond vocally, but her sobs subsided a little. She was listening. That had to be a good sign. Her shaking slowed, though it didn't stop. She looked up at him, eyes wet and large and dark.

Trapp slowly pulled his torn T-shirt away from his throat, revealing a scar that started just above his left collarbone and crossed his neck before dying on the right. It was more faded than it had once been, the scar tissue whiter than its initial, fiery red. It was splotched with darker, deeper circles where the rusted wire had dug in. He tried to forget that there was anyone in the room other than him and Nadia. Or that there were others listening in on the other side.

"My father did this to me when I was a boy," he said quietly, absentmindedly tracing the scar from left to right. "It almost killed me."

"What happened to him?" Nadia said shakily.

Unconsciously gritting his teeth, Trapp replied, "He won't hurt anybody else. I made sure of that."

Nadia's gaze focused intently on his own. It was as though

she was reaching deep into his soul, divining truth from artifice.

Trapp pushed away the memories that threatened to consume him. "Your husband, Omar, he hurts you, doesn't he." No question, just recognition passing from one victim to another. "And your sons."

Without once breaking eye contact, Nadia nodded. She spoke a single, breathy word. "Yes."

"Tell me about him."

"You know it already," she said. "He hits me. Beats me. Takes me at night."

She pulled her blanket upward, still staring intently at Trapp. He gestured at the translator to look away. She revealed a heavy, purple bruise on the lower part of her right thigh. Its edges were yellowed, but at the center was a dark, ugly pupil.

"He woke me this way three nights ago," she said, speaking freely for the first time as though it was a relief to be able to share her truth. "Because I hadn't taken the washing off the line. It was still wet. But that didn't matter to him."

"And your sons?"

Nadia's throat clenched. "He hurts them too. Not often. I can usually stop him."

"But not always," Trapp remarked, knowing that truth well.

"No."

He said nothing for several long seconds as he processed what she'd said. He wondered how interrogators did this day after day, week after week. Only a few minutes in and this conversation was already bringing memories to the surface that he'd long buried. It was the casualness with which Nadia referred to her marital rape that almost broke him.

"Will he take care of your son?"

She swallowed. "Omar is a cold man. He will look after Abdel—until he doesn't."

"When his own safety is threatened, you mean?"

"Or he sees some advantage in casting Abdel off."

More silence. Nadia broke it first. "Will you help me?"

Trapp was about to nod when he caught himself. He could not promise anything to this woman. Not because he didn't want to but because he knew how this worked. Nobody would greenlight a strike mission to save one Iraqi kid, not while a whole country was burning down with only so many firefighters to go around. And he couldn't lie to her and say that they would.

He danced around the question. "Do you know where your husband is?"

"Will you help me?" Nadia repeated forcefully. She was no longer wrapped up in a ball. She was practically vibrating with energy.

"I'll try."

"That's not good enough."

"I won't lie to you," Trapp said. "That other man, he would tell you whatever you wanted to hear. And it wouldn't mean shit. He's like your husband. Cold. Broken."

The translator sounded embarrassed to be in the room. "And you aren't?"

"I try not to be. I've killed, but I'm not a killer. There's a difference. I hope."

"If I tell you where Omar is, Abdel might get hurt."

"He might get hurt either way. All I can promise you is that if you tell me where Omar is, I'll do everything in my power to return Abdel to you. Most of us here are good people. We want to help, not hurt. That's all I can guarantee."

Nadia chewed over the statement, the indecision carved into her anguished face as she weighed up the competing claims to her son's life. Finally she reached her decision.

She bowed her head before she spoke. "He's been meeting with someone."

"Who?"

"I don't know his name. My husband would never share such things with me. But he's important. Powerful. Omar met him in the same place twice. Both times he came back happy."

Trapp frowned. "Happy how?"

"He didn't hit me," Nadia said plainly.

Trapp didn't waste breath on condolences. She was too strong for that. "And you know where these meetings took place?"

She nodded. "I do."

7

Trapp's stomach sank the second he exited the interrogation room. A gaggle of soldiers was standing in the hallway waiting for him. The Delta squad leader Breyer was one of them. The translator exited just behind Trapp and beat a hasty retreat—implicitly washing his hands of everything that had happened inside. He was left standing alone.

Sikorski was in the crowd and shot Trapp an apologetic grimace. Hook stood alongside him wearing a shit-eating grin. He looked like a kid that had just snitched to the principal on a schoolyard fight. Trapp itched to grab him by the throat a second time and teach him the lesson that he'd so obviously skipped out on as a child.

But he had more immediate problems to contend with.

"Sergeant," a cold—furious—voice hissed. "Do you care to tell me exactly what you were doing in there?"

With fatigue slowing his movements, Trapp snapped to attention. He stared directly ahead, fixing his gaze at a point on the wall opposite him rather than meeting Colonel Ruzzier's eye. Task Force Center's commanding officer was dressed in an olive-green Army T-shirt, tan camouflage pants, and running sneakers. He looked like he'd just rolled out of bed.

"Yes, sir."

"Well?"

"I was conducting an interrogation of the non-combatant we apprehended earlier this morning."

"Under whose authority?" Ruzzier said, his gaze burning into Trapp's skin, reminding him that he had almost no room for error. The CO was whip-smart. There would be no pulling the wool over his eyes.

He toyed with the idea of saying that the lieutenant had ordered him to attend an interrogation but rejected it. Frivolity wouldn't get him far with the colonel. "My own, sir."

"You don't have any authority!" Hook protested, both loudly and smugly. "Operators are allowed to observe. Encouraged, even. But the interrogations themselves are sacrosanct. Colonel, I demand that Sergeant Trapp is punished, and punished *severely* for this infraction. You need to make an example of him."

"Clear the hallway," Ruzzier said quietly, dismissing everybody who wasn't directly involved. "Not you, Sikorski. You stay. You too, Hook."

Trapp kept his expression completely impassive but almost cracked a smile at the hangdog look on Sikorski's face.

Once the hallway was empty, Ruzzier turned to the contractor. "Hook—shut the fuck up. When I require your input, I will ask for it. Did I just request it?"

With a sour, stunned look on his face, Hook shook his head.

"Then keep your mouth shut. You don't have the power to demand anything on this base. You are an asset, and increasingly not a useful one. If I was standing on ice as thin as the sheet beneath your feet, I would learn when to hold my tongue."

A long, heavy silence developed, but Ruzzier wasn't done. "Is that clear?"

"Yes, Colonel."

"Good. You're dismissed."

Hook turned slowly, utter disbelief etched on his face. Once he'd exited the hallway, leaving them alone, Ruzzier turned back to Trapp.

"Sergeant, Hook wasn't wrong. You do not have the authority to question prisoners without a trained interrogator in the room with you. More than that, I understand you assaulted a contractor. You could be court-martialed for that. Hell, maybe you should be. I can't accept that kind of insolence in my unit."

"No, sir."

"Do you intend to explain your actions?"

"I will accept whatever consequences you deem necessary, Colonel," Trapp said simply.

A ghost of a smile appeared on Ruzzier's face, though it was extinguished so quickly that Trapp wondered whether he'd imagined it.

"I'm very grateful." the officer said dryly. "But the thing about consequences, Sergeant, is that they apply whether or not you choose to accept them."

"Yes, sir."

"Do you have anything to say for yourself?"

"Not in my defense, sir."

"Quit talking in riddles, Sergeant," Ruzzier said. "I'm tired and not best disposed to waste my precious energy in deciphering them, especially when you are the reason I'm losing two of my allotted six hours of sleep tonight."

"Sir," Trapp said quickly, "I believe that Hook should be relieved of duty. His interrogations are... not fit for purpose. That's all."

"And you believe yours are better?"

Suspecting a trap, he didn't answer.

Ruzzier waited for a few seconds but didn't force the issue. He drummed his palm against his thigh. "I suppose it's lucky for you, Sergeant, that you got her to sing."

"Anybody could have, sir," Trapp said. That was the point.

"Except Hook?"

"Yes, sir."

Ruzzier bowed his head in thought for a second. "I suspect you're wrong about the first part, Sergeant. You're dismissed."

Trapp blinked. He hadn't expected that. "But what about the new targets? We need to hit them as soon as possible, while the intel is still good."

"Thank you for the primer on how to do my job, Sergeant Trapp. I wasn't sure I needed one, but you stepped in anyway. We'll exploit this intelligence, don't worry about that. You're a team player, right?"

With a sinking feeling in his stomach, Trapp nodded. "Yes, sir."

"And your squad has tomorrow night off?"

He frowned as he tried to work out what day it was before realizing that the colonel was correct. "Uh-huh."

"Then you won't mind giving up some of your precious time to assist with this operation?"

"Of course not."

"Good. Your guys can handle the security cordon. It's important work, Sergeant. Don't let me down."

As Colonel Ruzzier strode off, Trapp leaned against the nearest wall, closed his eyes, and let the back of his head thud against it. The CO had played him, there were no two ways about it. The entire base knew he favored the Delta squads and gave them the pick of the choicest missions. But Captain Myers was usually able to push back on the pressure from upstairs and ensure that his Rangers were able to hit the targets that their own intelligence generated.

Not this time.

The worst part of it was that his guys could use a quiet night. In his hotheaded rush to exploit the intelligence that Nadia had given up, he'd forgotten the most important part of leadership: to look out for the men under his care.

Trapp made a fist, his nails biting into his palm. Sikorski could really use a night off. His friend's easy manner was mistaken by many as a sign that he didn't feel the pressure of their work. But Trapp knew that wasn't true. The jokes were a release valve, and their increasing frequency was a sign that all wasn't well underneath the surface.

"Shit," he muttered.

"What's wrong, Sergeant?" a gruff voice asked.

His eyes snapped open to reveal Breyer by the door to the hallway. Trapp realized that the man must have been lingering this entire time. His next realization was that there was a mocking smile on the man's lips. For a moment, he felt his right fist clenching. Instead he turned away.

"I'm always here if you need me," Breyer called after him insincerely.

"Get bent," he replied through gritted teeth. Breyer was one of those guys who thought joining Delta meant he walked on water. And he never missed the chance to remind his perceived inferiors of their station in life.

"That's *get bent, Staff Sergeant.*"

"Whatever the hell you say."

8

"Leroy 5 is five mikes out from Objective Burnt Ridge, over."

"Copy, Leroy 5," a calm voice from Task Force Center's command operations room radioed back. "Your operation is go. Happy hunting."

Captain Alexis Chavez glanced down at the GPS unit on his Blackhawk's control console, its screen dimmed so that the small icon that represented his helicopter was just barely visible in the gloom. He adjusted the cyclic between his knees just a fraction of an inch, an alteration so small that its effects were barely noticeable—except to him.

This was Chavez's second deployment with the 160th SOAR, and he'd piloted missions just like this one so many times he figured he could probably drop the operators his bird was carrying onto a roof the size of a nickel with his eyes closed and running on half an hour's sleep. Still, he left nothing to chance, constantly monitoring the instruments in front of him, the sound of the powerful engine he was ultimately strapped into, the positions of the other three helicopters arrayed around his in the darkness, and even the faint smell of burned aviation fuel on the air.

"Leroy 5, tuck in a little tighter. Leroy 2 out."

"Leroy 5 copies," Chavez drawled, touching the throttle control and eking out another couple of knots. The chopper responded smoothly to his inputs, eating up about 30 yards before he pulled back and settled into his new position.

As he flew, he pictured how the next few moments would go. The flight of four helicopters would speed toward Objective Burnt Ridge—the building intelligence had identified as containing the target. The two Apache gunships would break away at the last second to take up firing positions on opposite sides of the structure. The two Blackhawks would spin on a dime around the building, bleeding speed and altitude until they dropped into a hover directly over the roof.

Almost before the makeover was over, the Delta operators would jump off the ramp onto the building. It was quicker and safer than fast roping, and Chavez knew he was plenty skilled as a pilot to give the shooters the steady platform they required. The second his crew chief confirmed they were free and clear, both Leroy choppers would bug out and maintain a holding position about a mile away from the objective to allow the Apaches clear fields of fire.

With luck, the night's mission would proceed without a single shot being fired. In truth, most operations went that way, even for the operators he ferried around night after night. If he had to guess, over 90 percent of the missions for which he flew ended with the bad guy being taken into custody without shooting back. Over the past couple of years, both Delta and the Rangers had gotten very good at hitting buildings before their targets even became aware. Often the first warning the bad guys had that they were in trouble was a flashlight shining at their eyes or the cold kiss of a pistol's muzzle thrust through their teeth.

"Objective is in sight, Leroy 5," his wingman stated over the radio.

"I see it," Chavez replied. He rolled his neck left and right to free any tension that might inhibit him at a key moment. There was none, but it was a ritual he'd adopted in his first deployment and which was now second nature. Irrationally, he now feared that the night he failed to carry it out would be the one in which disaster struck.

Better not risk it.

The four helicopters thundered over the final stretch. Chavez caressed the cyclic between his knees and prepared to execute the maneuver he'd modeled in his head. He was so focused on doing it right and doing it safely that he reacted half a second late to the bright white glow of an incoming missile's rocket motor in his night vision goggles.

A loud, urgent tone blared inside the Blackhawk's cockpit. An instant later, the radio net lit up with excited, strained chatter. "Leroy 2, Singer. Break, break, break."

Chavez had heard that tone a thousand times before, but always in the simulator. Still, despite his disbelief, he reacted just as he'd trained for, dragging the cyclic hard left and dumping brilliant red flares into the night sky. He pushed the throttle to its limit, urging his bird forward. His chest felt tight from the adrenaline now pumping through his veins, or maybe just the additional G forces from loading the Blackhawk's airframe far beyond the edge of its design envelope.

He craned his neck left and right in search of the incoming missile. Where the hell was it? That question was answered not even a fraction of a second later, when the SAM's infrared seeker locked on to the cloud of flares that he'd ejected and its warhead detonated.

"What the fuck," he breathed, eyes wide as he stared at the flame cloud in the night's sky. The insurgents had fired RPGs at helicopter insertions before, but never surface-to-air missiles. And definitely never at him.

The CMWS—or Common Missile Warning System— screamed a second time. Stunned by this turn of events, Chavez dropped his gaze to a green dial on his instrument panel. At the center of the display was a circular etched line that indicated his aircraft. A red warning light had now replaced the usual green on the right-hand side of the display.

"Leroy 5," he said, his voice suddenly clipped. "Singer, defending. 3 o'clock."

Singer was the brevity code for an enemy surface-to-air missile. Those words had never crossed his lips before, at least not for real.

"I see it, Leroy 5," a voice—he wasn't sure who amid the madness—said over the radio. "Punching flares."

"We've got another launch," a third voice said, the man's voice raw with strain. "Singer at my six."

Chavez punched the flare ejection button built into his cyclic with the energy of a madman as he jerked the control left and right and bled off as much altitude as he dared. How many times had he crashed in the simulator in just this scenario as a trainee—successfully dodging an incoming missile only to hit the dirt because he'd lost situational awareness in the chaos?

As he pumped another set of flares out into the darkness, briefly seeing their glow before he jinked his bird, Chavez thought he heard one of the operators in the back swearing. That had to be impossible over the amount of noise that the chopper's engine was throwing out, but he would've sworn to it in court all the same.

"Fuck, fuck, fuck," he said over and over again as he manipulated the cyclic and as the last of his flares ran dry. "Come on, fucking *come on!*"

The second missile's warhead broke through the first cloud of chaff, its seeker not fooled by the tiny strands of aluminum-coated fibers floating on an upward thermal, only to detonate as it encountered the second. Chavez's hands trembled on his controls as he took stock of the fact that he was still alive. That they were all still alive. He dropped his head back and screamed something unintelligible into the blackness, pumping his fist over and over and over again.

The voice of the pilot of one of the Apache gunships instantly sluiced cold water over his elation. "Viper 2 is hit, say again Viper 2 is hit. I'm losing power. I'm going to have to put her down."

9

"What the hell was that?"

The Stryker armored vehicle's radio operator dropped the headset away from his ear with a look of utter disbelief on his face. The man's tone was so stunned that it even cut through Trapp's self-pitying reverie as he blackly contemplated the likelihood of disciplinary action.

"Was what?" he asked, giving voice to the other members of his fire team, who were seated alongside him in the Stryker's passenger compartment.

It was a tight, uncomfortable fit with all their gear, but at least the vehicle wasn't completely full. Three other vehicles, altogether containing two full squads of Rangers, were parked as part of the operation's quick reaction force about two klicks from Objective Burnt Ridge.

"I think the helicopters just got hit," the operator said.

"Hit with what?"

"Missiles," the man said, lifting the headset back to his ear to listen. "Shit, it's all going to hell out there. One of the Apaches took a hit for sure. It's going down."

Trapp formed a fist and punched down on his thigh, dispelling the thoughts of his own predicament for good. "The pilots?"

"Alive."

"Then let's go get them," Trapp said. "They'll be sitting ducks out there."

The operator held up his finger to forestall him, then shook his head. "No, the lieutenant wants us to hit Burnt Ridge. Now."

"You're shitting me," Sikorski exclaimed. "Those assholes are cooking off missiles like it's a Fourth of July party, and you're telling me the brass want us to go kick out their barbecue?"

"That's the job, Sikorski," Trapp said. He slapped the side of the Stryker to burn off some of the adrenaline pumping through his veins, rather than with any great expectation that the driver would hear. At any rate, the armored vehicle's powerful engine first coughed, then rumbled into life.

"What's the plan?" the Polish-American said plaintively over the loud grumble as the heavy vehicle started to edge forward.

"There is no plan," Trapp replied, scanning his rifle to check that all was in order before quickly passing an eye over the other members of his fire team. Nothing looked out of place.

"Yeah, well you see, that's the problem," Sikorski fired back, the ghost of a smile on his lips. "We were supposed to be the icing, not the whole damn soufflé."

"Do you put icing on a soufflé?" the radio operator asked, cocking his head to one side and in the process rattling his helmet against a thick steel reinforcing bar that ran horizontally along the troop compartment. "Dammit."

"How the hell should I know?" Sikorski said. "I ain't no cook."

"Baker," Trapp remarked, raising his voice to yell over the sound of the Stryker's engine and the rattling of its built-by-the-lowest-bidder chassis as the armored vehicle accelerated toward danger.

"Huh?"

"You bake a soufflé, you don't cook it," Trapp said. "So it stands to reason you'd be called a baker."

"What about a pastry architect?" Sikorski suggested.

"I think you're overthinking it."

Sikorski was about to fire back another quip when the squad's radio net squawked. "Sgt. Trapp, how copy?"

It was the lieutenant.

"I hear you sir, over," Trapp said, his demeanor immediately darkening as the demands of the mission reasserted themselves.

"I want you to breach."

"Understood, sir. Which entrance?"

"No time," the officer barked, raising his voice to be heard over the rattling of his own command vehicle. "Make one."

"Copy," Trapp said. "Out."

"Make one?" Sikorski said disbelievingly. "With me and what excavator? This assault ain't a surprise anymore. The second we get there, the bad guys will light us up. He didn't even have any ideas. *Make one*. Sure. I'll get right on it."

"Can it, Sikorski," Trapp said, closing his eyes to help him concentrate. The vague outlines of the missing plan were beginning to form in his mind. "I got an idea."

Sikorski groaned, reaching up and placing his flat palm on the roof for support as they were flung about in the rear of the fast-moving Stryker. "Now I'm really worried," he said. "The reason we're here in the first place is because you had a bright idea."

Trapp's eyes snapped open, and he shot his friend—and

subordinate—a grim glare that silenced him instantly. Then, with a mild twinkle in his eye, he said, "I never said you were going to like it."

He held down the radio transmit button and relayed his plan to the command vehicle, making sure that it was repeated back to him before he signed off. They were now just over thirty seconds out from the Burnt Ridge compound. Sikorski was right about one thing—the bad guys would be well and truly awake by now. Hell, they'd been lying in wait at the start of this. But that was where the private went wrong.

It wasn't the worst time to press home an attack—it was the best. The insurgents likely thought they'd been victorious. Either they were in the process of bugging out or they would be jubilant as they celebrated their victory over the hated Americans. Either way, the last thing they would expect would be an attack from the ground.

And certainly not one with the flavor that Trapp intended to impart.

In a cramped section at the front of the true compartment, the Stryker's weapons operator was hunched over a glowing screen and a joystick that looked like it'd been taken from an arcade machine.

Catching the man's attention, Trapp said, "The moment you get that building in your sights, lay down suppressing fire. There's nothing behind for several miles. You don't have to worry about civilians. Just keep the bad guys pinned down. And then hold on tight."

The weapons operator looked back at him like he'd lost his mind. Trapp shrugged to himself. Maybe he was right.

"Twenty seconds," Trapp called out, relaying one further piece of information from the driver. "Make sure you're strapped in. Otherwise this is going to hurt."

The entire Stryker shook as the M2 Browning heavy

machine gun slaved to the Stryker's remote weapon system opened up. Its operator fired in bursts of half a dozen rounds, peppering the exterior walls of Objective Burnt Ridge with holes the size of a man's fist.

"Ten seconds."

"Make one," Sikorski muttered darkly, cinching his harness tight.

The rumble of the machine gun was relentless as Trapp counted off the last few seconds out loud. He couldn't even tell whether his voice was audible, but he did it anyway.

"Five."

"Four."

"Three."

"Two—"

The Stryker's low, arrow-shaped nose impacted the compound's outer wall a second early. The twenty-ton vehicle was traveling at sixty miles an hour, which was a math problem that the wall didn't have time to figure out before it crumbled and the Stryker punched through.

Sikorski groaned as his harness tightened around his chest, stopping his body from smashing itself like a ragdoll against the steel chassis but doing nothing to support his neck, which snapped in whiplash fashion to the left, then the right. Trapp grunted at the force of the impact as his own body was wrenched viciously to the side as the Stryker came to a dead stop.

The armored vehicle lodged itself halfway in and halfway out of the wall. Above them, invisible chunks of brick and mortar rattled the Stryker's armored chassis, ringing the ears of those inside.

"Reverse!" Trapp yelled, accompanying the command with a series of fruitless hand gestures with his left as he unbuckled his harness with his right. The driver gunned the armored vehicle's engine, producing a loud shriek as the wheels spun underneath, dragging a piece of dislodged rubble against the undercarriage.

The Stryker lurched a few inches, then ground to a stop. The driver switched directions, fed the vehicle a hefty helping of gas, and punched it back through the hole it had generated in the wall in his attempt to work the unwieldy fighting vehicle free. A fresh cascade of rubble clattered against the armored skin, pounding with the speed and intensity of a rock drummer at a stadium concert.

As the rattling slowed, the driver switched directions once again and was finally able to punch back out of the hole that he'd created. It took a few more seconds, but the Stryker finally pulled itself free of the breaching hole.

"Okay, let's move!" Trapp said, tapping the other members of his fire team as he passed them. He dropped his night vision goggles down over his eyes. "Stay low, move fast. Hooah."

"Hooah," they repeated as if by rote, conditioned by years of service.

Trapp wrestled the Stryker's outer door open and jumped out in the same movement, immediately lifting his rifle to the crook of his shoulder and dropping to one knee to cover his team's exit. Around him, the three other Strykers were skidding to a halt, and small groups of men were beginning to ape his movements.

"Let's go," Trapp called out the second the last of his team exited the safety of the true compartment. Raising his voice, he yelled, "Bravo breaching."

There was no time to work out a more detailed assault plan. He guessed that the reason Task Force Center hadn't waited to reassemble and redeploy the primary strike team was the risk of allowing a safe house packed with loose surface-to-air missiles to disappear into the wind. The corollary, of course was that this placed him and the men he was fighting with at even greater risk.

But that was the job.

"Sikorski, point," he ordered.

"Got it," the soldier replied, all business now. He clambered over the rubble and threw himself against the edge of the hole that the Stryker had gouged into Burnt Ridge's outer wall, resting against it with his left shoulder and sweeping his rifle left and right across the dark, dusty expanse it had revealed.

"I see a courtyard," he said. "Looks empty."

"Alpha coming up behind," a fresh voice shouted.

Knowing he had backup, Trapp made the decision to move in. Though he would've made it anyway. "Then let's go."

He sucked in a lungful of thick, dusty air as he followed Sikorski into the compound, one hand on the soldier's left shoulder and another soldier's on his own.

"I've got a door to my left," Sikorski called out. "Nothing to the right."

"Got it," Trapp replied, stepping sideways to cover his friend. He swept his head side to side, scanning the front of the building to make sure that the private hadn't missed anything. There was only one window, and it was boarded up.

He raised his head to look at the roof. "Oh, shit. Duck!"

The cry probably saved Sikorski's life. The private's training took command, and he hit the deck a second later. A stream of bullets chewed up the patch of air he had just been occupying.

"Suppressing fire," Trapp called out, squeezing his trigger and sending a hail of metal toward the flat roof of the building at the back of the courtyard. He'd seen only one insurgent up there but two muzzle flashes. "We got multiple tangos. Two for sure, maybe more."

"Grenade!" a voice called out. Trapp barely saw the tiny soda can-sized shape flying through the air but instantly calculated that he was too far away to do anything about it. It was heading right for Sikorski.

The private was still on the ground but scrambled instinctively away as the grenade landed, then bounced toward him.

"Shit!" he yelled, his voice strangled and high-pitched. He kicked out from his awkward position lying on his ass on the ground, but managed to boot the explosive with surprising force, sending it skidding across the dusty ground to the other side of the compound.

Trapp threw himself to the ground, covering his ears with his palms, and waited. It didn't take long. The grenade detonated with a loud crump, sending a wall of heat rolling out, then a shower of dust and earth as a hail of shrapnel impacted the ground and walls all around them. He rolled onto his back, aiming his weapon even as he struggled to breathe and fired half a magazine up at the roof.

"Somebody get some indirect fire on that roof," he shouted, raising his voice to be heard over the ringing in his own ears as he scrambled back to his feet.

"Way ahead of you," a laconic voice replied. A Ranger stepped out of the dust and the mayhem, a grenade in either hand. The pin on the first was already missing, but the spoon was pinned to the frag casing. The man relaxed his grip, waited a moment, then lifted his arm as though he was tossing a baseball and looped the grenade up and over the lip of the roof.

It detonated the second it disappeared from sight.

"That's how it's done!" Sikorski whooped, the adrenaline still clearly pumping from his brush with death.

The Ranger followed the first blast up with a second, more carefully placed throw that appear to land somewhere toward the back of the roof. A dozen soldiers were now in the building's courtyard, their weapons aimed upward. A final crackle of gunfire erupted, pock-marking the upper part of the bleached, sandy building and sending a fine dust coursing downward. After that, it was over. Anyone on top of that roof was either too dead or too injured to fight. Either that, or they'd made the sensible decision that it wasn't worth testing the Rangers below them.

An operator with a large black shotgun stepped through the crowd. He unshouldered the weapon and aimed its muzzle at the lock. The shotgun had at some point been spray-painted in desert tan but was now so worn with use that its most recent coat of paint was almost gone.

Trapp stepped forward, flanking the man on the right-hand side. Sikorski did the same to his left. The rest of the fire team filled in behind.

"Breach," Trapp said, his throat thick with dust. He coughed and wiped the back of his arm roughly across his lips, biting back the urge to do it again.

A loud blast rang out as the Ranger with the shotgun wasted no time. A hole the size of a dinner plate appeared where the door handle had been. The door swung back a few inches before coming to a stop. It didn't stay there long. The same operator drew himself back and unleashed a powerful kick, aiming his heel just above the hole he'd created.

Sikorski danced past him, sweeping his rifle left and right. Trapp followed. Inside, the building was a simple structure. They had entered a kind of living room, in which the only furniture was a low dining table that sat only a foot or so off the ground. It was surrounded by cushions on the ground in the Bedouin style. The wall to the left was decorated with a hanging rug, though the details were impossible to make out through Trapp's night vision goggles.

Sikorski's voice rang out loud and unbowed, all thoughts of his earlier tangle with fate seemingly forgotten as he moved toward an interior archway that led into the next room. "Clear!"

As Trapp joined him on the other side, he realized that the building's layout was simple: two rooms on the lower floor and the staircase to the second floor in the far room—which was also empty. Inside it, a rifle was leaning against the wall, and on the floor right by it was a tray stacked with used coffee cups and a plate of some kind of flat, sweet cake.

"Looks like we disturbed them," he muttered.

"Coffeepot's still glowing," Sikorski said, referencing the white-hot outline it was giving off in his thermal goggles. "I think you're right."

"Let's take the stairs," Trapp said as behind him half a dozen more Rangers entered the building.

"You got it."

Blood pounded in Trapp's ears as they crossed the second room. As far as he could tell, there was no sign of a basement. The floor felt solid, as though it was constructed of concrete or hardened mud rather than wooden planks. Neither could he see any evidence of an escape tunnel—or even any place one might be hidden.

He joined Sikorski at the foot of the stairs. They were simple, wooden, and looked rickety as all hell. "Great," he said.

"I'll go first," Sikorski said softly, glancing up and down Trapp's frame with an expression that suggested he didn't like the odds of the staircase remaining standing if they both took it at the same time.

"That's not—"

"Negotiable," he finished smoothly. "Moving."

Trapp ground his jaw tightly shut, holding his breath until Sikorski reached the top and pivoted to his right. He started up the second the stairwell was empty. It creaked and swayed underneath him, vindicating his friend's decision to go it alone.

Before he was able to make it up and join him, Sikorski called out "Clear" once again.

The second floor wasn't partitioned. It was one large space. Several thin mattresses lined the ground, all empty. Trapp's stomach tightened as he saw a small pile of children's clothing on one of them. He hardened his mind, knowing he had to focus on the task at hand. He swept the room, searching for the exits. A ladder was mounted on the wall at the far end of the room, leading up to a trapdoor that was open.

"Wish we could get some eyes in the sky up there," Sikorski said as they approached, staying a few feet back in case anyone unfriendly was still alive up there.

"I've got a better idea," Trapp said, unhooking a grenade from his vest. "Frag out!"

He waited a few seconds for the cry to echo—and be repeated—throughout the building before he pulled the pin and lobbed it onto the roof. Before it detonated, there were no cries of concern. Just silence.

And then an explosion that rocked the already damaged building.

"Okay, maybe not a *better* idea." Trapp grinned.

"Hey." Sikorski shrugged. "If it's stupid but gets the job done, it ain't stupid."

"No arguments here," he replied as he climbed the ladder.

They emerged onto a roof on which they found three very dead insurgents. Each had been ripped apart by the hail of grenades. Trapp radioed that the building was secure and saw that the Rangers below were already pushing out and forming a security cordon. As far as he could see from this vantage point, it was pointless. There was nobody out there.

"This place looks like a bust," Sikorski said, slinging his weapon. "And we missed the kid."

"Abdel," Trapp muttered. "His name is Abdel."

He pushed up his goggles and pulled out a flashlight. He clicked it on and swept the beam across the rooftop. On top of it he saw several expended launch tubes—from the missiles they'd heard so much about—as well as a shower of brass casings that skittered underfoot as he paced.

He played the beam of the flashlight across the face of one of the dead insurgents. Several pieces of shrapnel had entered underneath the man's chin, though the proximate cause of death was most likely due to the fact he no longer had a stomach.

Trapp walked closer to the body and dropped to one knee. He focused the beam on a tattoo on the man's shoulder that depicted a military unit badge. In particular, an *Iranian* unit insignia. "Besides, I'm not so sure about that."

10

A knock rattled the flimsy wooden door to Trapp's bedroom, which wasn't any grander than a prison cell. A corkboard was attached to the wall above his cot, but he was still to decorate it several months into his deployment.

"Coming," Trapp said, sighing as he rolled out of bed. He had just gotten comfy—or as comfy as it was possible to get on a cot made for men half a foot shorter than he was. He flicked the light switch as he stood up, and the room's bare bulb started to hum as it filled the space with a harsh, unpleasant halogen glow.

Eyelids sagging from exhaustion, he almost didn't recognize the familiar, moustachioed face of Captain Myers as he pulled back the door. "Sir? Are you—"

"Lost?" Myers chuckled. "Not exactly. Though all these doors kinda look the same. I woke up Muniz by accident before I reached you. He wasn't pleased."

"No sir," Trapp said, too tired to come up with anything more substantial. "Can I help you with something?"

"You're wondering why I'm standing in front of your bedroom door at six in the morning?"

"Something like that," Trapp admitted.

"You did good out there tonight, Sergeant," Myers said. "But that's not why I'm here. It seems your particular set of skills has been requested."

"Requested how?"

"To interrogate the female prisoner again. From what I saw, you built up quite a rapport with her. This is a fast-moving situation. The brass is taking a keen interest in our little problem down here, and they want answers."

Trapp reflexively glanced at his wrist, forgetting that his watch was lying on the room's small desk. "Now, sir?"

"That's what the colonel wants. I guess an Apache getting shot down has a way of focusing the mind. She's being brought to the interrogation wing as we speak."

He nodded before the words fully processed in his mind, then caught himself. "Wait, is she—was she—in a cell?"

Myers frowned. "This isn't a hotel, Sergeant. Where else would we keep her?"

"With her son? The cells are no place for a kid."

"They're clean and safe," the captain protested with the defensiveness that suggested he knew that Trapp was right.

"I said what I said, sir."

Running his fingers through his hair, Myers's tone became short. "What is it you want, Trapp?"

"To have her moved somewhere more comfortable, sir. I'm no bleeding heart, but if you want her to talk, I'm guessing the best way is to get her thinking we're on her side."

"We are!"

"We're using her, sir," Trapp said, customarily clear-eyed about the situation. "And she knows it just as well as I do. It's just that she doesn't have any other choice. Maybe if she works with us, she gets lucky and we save her other boy. There's one other thing I'll need, sir."

A muscle flickered on Myers's jaw. Trapp guessed that he was walking on thin ice, but he felt a moral clarity about the situation that he sensed that the captain recognized also.

"What is it, Sergeant?"

"A female translator."

"That I can arrange," Myers said before continuing with a hint of sarcasm, "Do you have any ideas where I can find the local Four Seasons? A suite might be hard to rustle up at this time of night, but I'll do what I can."

Trapp shrugged. "Where do they put up members of Congress when they come for a photo opportunity? That should be comfortable enough. And Nadia deserves it a hell of a lot more than they do."

NADIA'S youngest son was sleeping on her lap when Trapp entered the VIP apartment. It wasn't much fancier than a small-town motel room, but it was a palace compared to the austere cell they'd been keeping her in before. The only clue that she was still a prisoner was the military policeman posted to stand guard outside.

The translator followed him in.

"I'm sorry for visiting so late," Trapp said. "It's been a busy night."

His mouth tasted of cheap coffee, and he wished he hadn't drunk it, despite the pervasive fatigue that ran throughout his body. In his left hand, he held three photographs, blown up to legal pad size and still warm from the printer. The fingers of his right were clutched around a small pile of cloth, which he kneaded subconsciously as he waited for the interpreter to finish.

Nadia looked up at him, not seeming surprised by his presence. Her eyes were a bloodshot red. She ran her fingers metronomically through her son's hair. His breath caught momentarily, and she looked down in what seemed like near panic, relaxing only when the smooth movement of his diaphragm resumed.

"I couldn't sleep," she said via the translator. "And then they brought me here."

"I thought it would be more comfortable," Trapp said. "You can stay here as long as—" He broke off, not knowing how to continue.

Perceptively, Nadia caught his eye. "Am I free to go?"

"At some point," Trapp replied. "You're not suspected of any crime."

"But if I tried to walk out of here right this moment, what would happen to me?"

Trapp shrugged awkwardly. "I'm sorry. I can't answer that."

Nadia looked down, her shoulders hunching from a combination of exhaustion and mental strain. "You didn't find my son."

Trapp glanced at the bundle of clothing in his right hand. It had been bagged when the house was swept for intelligence. He swallowed, not wanting to inflict this pain on her, then thrust his arm forward. "Is this what he was wearing when he was taken?"

She snatched the clothes away from him and started to pick them over, running the fabric through her fingers, then bringing it up to her nose to smell. When she was finally done, her eyes were wet with tears. She glowered at him. "You were too late!"

"I'm still looking. We got close, but not close enough. If you help me, maybe we can do better."

"What do you want?" Nadia said, clutching her son's clothes to her chest and rocking back and forth, the movements slight so as not to wake up her other child. "I told you everything I know. He could be anywhere!"

"Can I sit?" Trapp asked, gesturing at the sofa beside her.

She shrugged listlessly, her earlier burst of energy seeming to have faded.

"I want to show you some photos. I need to warn you that they aren't pretty," Trapp said, keeping the images face down until the translator was done.

"My son?"

"No. Men who were killed when we went looking for him," Trapp said, knowing that he was being economical with the truth. They had gone after the missiles, not Nadia's child.

Nadia ground her jaw, seemingly chewing something over in her mind. Finally she spoke. "Will you tell me something?"

"Of course." Trapp nodded.

"If my son had been in the house where you found his clothes, would he have been in any danger?"

Trapp knew that this was a dangerous moment. Perhaps a more practiced interrogator could've danced around the question, but he wasn't one of those. So he went with honesty instead.

"Yes. We are careful. We train for this every single day. But there is always risk."

Nadia bowed her head, dropping her chin all the way to her chest, and fell silent. She remained that way for almost a minute, during which a tension built inside the room. Twice Trapp opened his mouth to break the silence, but he stopped himself both times, unwilling to risk the progress he'd made so far.

"Show me these men," she finally said.

Trapp nodded, wondering why she'd acquiesced but not wanting to ask. Instead, he flipped over the trio of images and raised the first in front of her. They didn't have an identity for any of the three men who had died in the raid on Burnt Ridge, though their fingerprints and biometrics had been taken and were being run through every database known to man. If they'd been picked up before, or if any intelligence agency had a file on them, they would know before long. But in Iraq in 2007, most militants were unknown—just ordinary men who had picked up a weapon to resist the hated American invaders.

Nadia shook her head. "I don't know him."

"That's fine," Trapp said smoothly, turning over the next.

Again Nadia demurred. "Him either."

Feeling his hope that this conversation would reveal anything productive draining away, Trapp set the second photograph down on the sofa. He picked up the last without much expectation. It was of the man he'd examined on the rooftop, the one with the tattooed shoulder.

"What about him?"

Nadia started shaking her head even before she saw the photograph, but when he placed it in front of her, she froze. The face belonged to the corpse that sported a tattoo of an Iranian Revolutionary Guard unit badge.

Trapp straightened, feeling a hint of electricity in the room. All thoughts of tiredness faded from his mind. He couldn't even taste the coffee anymore. "You've seen him before."

She didn't say anything in return. Trapp glanced at the translator, wondering if he'd misjudged her reaction, but the woman only shrugged.

"Nadia?"

Finally she stirred, though she did not look away from the photograph once. She spoke quietly, as if afraid of being overheard. "My husband offered me to that man once. A long time ago."

Trapp thought he must've heard the translator wrong, but the expression on Nadia's face put him right. Nausea rose in his stomach. He wished he didn't have to pry further into this woman's pain. "When?"

"Maybe two years. When he first got himself tangled up with those animals. That man scares me."

"You know his name?" Trapp asked, leaning forward with interest he wished he could disguise—or simply not feel at all.

"No. But I've seen him many times before. Always at night. He would drive to the border with my husband. Sometimes they would bring back weapons and explosives and leave them on our farm overnight. I tried to argue with Omar because of this many times, but—"

Trapp didn't ask why she had stopped.

"The Iranian border?" he asked.

"Of course."

He turned to the final document in his hands. When he'd entered the room, he'd thought it was a long shot. But now he sensed that Nadia might be able to help him unravel the whole puzzle. Along with the expended missile tubes and Abdel's clothes, the intelligence people combing through Burnt Ridge had found a number of links—mostly maps and hand-shredded documents—to a small settlement located about 10 miles from the border with Iran.

"Have you heard of a place called Ali Daud?"

Nadia's gaze flashed up. The name clearly meant something to her. "Why?"

"It's possible your son might have been taken there. But it's a long shot."

"Omar's father was born there. He died four years ago. But we never sold his house. There was no market after the invasion. And then Omar didn't want to sell it. Maybe that's where he went with the man you showed me."

"Could you identify it for me on a map?"

She nodded, and Trapp set one down in front of her. She looked at it, frowning, then reoriented it to her satisfaction. When she was done, she traced her finger down one of the roads into the village, briefly closing her eyes, her eyelids flickering as she translated her memories into their cartographic representations. They opened again, and her finger stopped on a small house in the dead center of the settlement. "Here."

"Thank you," Trapp said, imbuing his words with as much gratitude as he felt. "I'll do everything I can to—"

"I know," she said. A tear rolled down her cheek. She glanced down at her sleeping child, then asked, "Is that everything? I'm tired."

He nodded and made to leave, wishing there was more he could do for her. As he reached the door, Trapp stopped so suddenly the translator bumped into him. He turned back, frowning. "Nadia, can I ask you something?"

"I've told you everything I know," she said, spreading her hands helplessly. "At least, all I think I know."

"It's not about that. Why did you keep talking to me when I told you that your son would've been in danger?"

Nadia kept quiet for a long time, staring directly into his gaze. "Because you didn't lie."

11

After the late-night interrogation, Trapp nominally had the chance of catching about five hours of sleep before the regularly scheduled midday briefing. In reality, he managed about three. The rest of that time, he tossed and turned, going over the information Nadia had given him again and again.

There was something wrong about this entire situation, or at least his subconscious mind thought that way. The problem was he had no idea *what*.

As he filed into the briefing room, clutching a cup of coffee in his left hand and a ham and cheese croissant in his right, Sikorski fell in alongside him.

"I hear you did good, Sergeant," he said.

Flakes of pastry ran down Trapp's chin as he took a bite from the croissant. He washed it down with a large swig of over-heated coffee, then took a deep breath to cool his mouth. Good-naturedly, he said, "You hear everything."

Sikorski tapped his nose conspiratorially. "That's what they want you to think."

Then he burst out laughing. "No, seriously. I hear we're gearing up for a hell of an op tonight. If we get lucky, historians will write books about this for decades to come."

"Or unlucky," Trapp remarked.

"What you mean?"

"*Black Hawk Down* would've been a real crappy story if the bad guys never took a lucky shot."

Sikorski cocked his head to one side as he thought it over. "Yeah, you're probably right. I hadn't thought of it that way."

They took their seats a second before Captain Myers entered the room, stood to attention, then sat back down. Like always, the introductory slide for a PowerPoint presentation was being beamed by projector onto a screen on the wall.

"I'll get right into it," Myers said, picking up a laser pointer. He tapped a button on it, and the next slide appeared on the wall. A face appeared on screen, blown up a dozen times from the picture that Nadia had recognized earlier that morning.

"This is Arash Taheri. He was killed yesterday on the raid on Burnt Ridge. Over the last twelve hours, we have been able to identify this individual as a"—he made quotation marks with his fingers—"*former* member of the Iranian Revolutionary Guard Corps. By which I mean he is, or was, up to his neck in activities that we can be sure are most definitely contrary to coalition objectives in Iraq."

Myers tapped another button, and an image of a much younger Taheri appeared on screen. "This is the only other picture we have of him, but we're sure it's the same guy. And there's more good news," he said sardonically.

The next slide appeared. "Our friend here is a close and known associate of Major Hossein Jafari, a senior operational commander within the Quds Force. I don't need to spell out to any of you guys what these guys are about. Suffice it to say that they are not the kind of guys we want operating on our patch."

Staff Sergeant Breyer raised his hand. Trapp bristled at the sight of him, irked by their last interaction, but forced himself to simmer down.

"Captain," he said slowly, "is this the same Hossein Jafari that we were briefed on a few weeks back? Because that seems like a real unlikely coincidence."

"We are in agreement, Breyer," Myers said, putting a picture of the Iranian officer on-screen. "It seems that our intelligence that Major Jafari was active inside Iraq has been proven correct. At present our working theory is that he's in our neck of the woods to ink weapons supply deals with insurgent groups like the Sheibani Network. The Iranians don't seem to care whether they supply Sunni or Shia outfits, just so long as the weapons get used to hit *us*."

"The enemy of my enemy," Breyer muttered.

"Something like that," Myers agreed.

Trapp stared at the screen with bleary eyes and rubbed his chin. If he hadn't known that Jafari was a commander with a brutal and storied history, he might have mistaken him for a history professor. But maybe there was something in the man's eyes that told a different story.

The sense he'd had before that something was wrong with this story was blaring even louder now. The Iranians didn't need to send a senior commander into Iraq just to seal a weapons supply deal. Hell, the very fact that Omar and Taheri had been doing shuttle runs to the border proved that Iranian munitions already flowed easily into the country.

So why come in person?

"Thanks to Sergeant Trapp over here," Myers continued, pointing at him from the briefing stage, "we have successfully ascertained that Omar Al-Hakim, the insurgent who escaped our raid a couple of nights back, owns a property in the village of Ali Daud, a stone's throw from the Iranian border. If there is a further supply of Misagh-1 missiles, it's possible that that's where they are stashed. Interdicting these weapons before they are able to spread more widely within the country is currently Task Force Center's primary—and only—concern. All other operations are on hold until we take this network down, understood?"

A grumble of agreement sounded across the room.

"Good. Because if we fuck up—or if more than a handful of these missiles have made it in country—then air mobility for all coalition forces in Iraq is going to be severely curtailed for the foreseeable future. Ladies, it's our job to make sure that doesn't happen."

Trapp wasn't really listening. He stared instead at the image on screen, drinking in every crevice and blemish on the Iranian commander's face, then the eyes, as if he could glean a hint as to the man's intentions just by looking at him.

"The good news is that we have recent aerial imagery of Ali Daud, courtesy of a Predator overflight at 0900," Myers said, putting it onto the screen with another click from his handheld remote. A small laser dot wobbled over the over-head surveillance shot before resolving over the same building that Nadia had identified just a few hours earlier. It was an impressive testament to the extent of American recon capabilities that such detailed imagery was available so quickly.

"The drone's operators observed a civilian car entering our target compound—from now on referred to as Red Buffalo—approximately fifteen minutes into their reconnaissance flight. Two men exited the vehicle and entered this building," he said, waving the laser dot over the only structure within the small compound, a two-story brick building about the same size as the one that Trapp had assaulted the previous night.

"The plan is to hit Red Buffalo at 0100 tomorrow morning. All operators are to report back here at 1800 for a full mission briefing, which will be refined over the course of this afternoon.

At present, I intend to employ Delta's Bravo Troop as the primary strike element."

Trapp glanced at Breyer, who nodded as if the decision was obvious.

Asshole.

"We have to work under the assumption that the missiles are being stored at this location. That being the case, an air assault is a no-go. We're going to have to go in on foot."

Another click and a topographical map appeared on screen.

"Ali Daud sits right here, on top of the first of a pair of bends in the Alwand River. It's not entirely clear from the surveillance shots, but we think there might be several boats tied up here under the tree line. Ranger Squads Bravo and Charlie will be waiting in four fast attack boats to cut off any retreat from this direction.

"Bravo Troop will split into two elements, Echo and Fox, along with two sniper pairs named Golf and Hotel. Golf will move to this position, a water tower on the northeast corner of the village, while Hotel gets themselves set up on top of this barn to the southwest. Both locations offer sufficient elevation to provide overwatch and clear fields of fire. The sniper teams will move into position 30 minutes before the main assault. Any questions?"

Breyer languidly raised his arm.

"Go ahead," Myers said, dropping the hand holding the laser pointer to his side and rolling his shoulder in its socket with a sigh of relief. Trapp hid a smile, wondering if the officer would put himself in for a Purple Heart.

"What do we know about the village? Any known insurgent activity?"

The same question had occurred to Trapp. Ali Daud probably wasn't big enough to qualify as truly urban combat, but it sure as hell wasn't an empty field. There were dozens of locations for bad guys to hide out and open fire on the attackers.

Worse still, only one road led to the village before breaking off into two lanes that ran through it at opposite ends. A single spotter posted a mile away from the settlement and equipped with a Motorola radio handset would be able to give any defenders ample time to prepare for an attack.

"Nothing since the invasion. It's just not on our radar. Seems peaceful. Mostly Shia, and it looks like they've kept themselves to themselves. I guess the fact that we are going in at all indicates they have some latent support for Iranian-backed Shia militant groups, but nothing kinetic."

Breyer nodded. "Let's hope it stays that way."

Myers continued with his briefing. "Echo and Fox will come off the highway as a single convoy in Pandur armored vehicles before splitting into their respective elements. Echo will travel down this lane," he said, waving the laser dot over the right hand of the two roads through Ali Daud, before shifting to the other, "and Fox this one. Both elements will converge on Red Buffalo at exactly 0120 hours and proceed with the assault."

Raising his arm a second time, Breyer asked, "Why not civilian vehicles? SUVs, maybe. It's less likely that our cover will be blown that way."

"Force protection," Myers replied. "My decision, and it's non-negotiable, Staff Sergeant. The IED risk on the main highway is off the charts. I'm not putting twenty-five of my best operators in tin cans and giving some Iraqi shithead with an artillery shell an opportunity to blow you guys to hell."

Breyer nodded, clearly unhappy but not enough to challenge the decision. Trapp, to his dismay, found he kind of agreed with the insufferable asshole's tactical read on the situation.

"Any questions?" Myers said. "Like I said, this operational plan will be refined by 1800. But if any of you guys have any thoughts, now is the time."

Trapp studied the surveillance shot of Ali Daud. There was

still something bugging him about this whole situation. The operational plan was good—with the obvious caveat that he would have rather assaulted from the air than the ground. There were good reasons why it was usually done that way, after all.

Then again, maybe getting shot down wasn't such a hot idea.

"Sergeant?" Myers said, pointing at him.

With a start, Tripp realized that his arm had migrated into the air without him even really noticing. He thought about backing out, but that wasn't really his style.

Screw it.

"Are we sure we didn't miss anything at Burnt Ridge?" he asked, raising an eyebrow.

"Like what?" Myers frowned.

"I'm not sure exactly," he admitted. "But something about this situation doesn't ring true to me. If we're dealing with an active Iranian intelligence cell, wouldn't we expect them to be a little less... sloppy? They must've known we tracked them once. Why leave intelligence at Burnt Ridge and give us an opportunity to do it a second time?"

Breyer shifted in his seat and turned to look at Trapp. "Because we hit them too quickly. We got inside their decision loop. Or did you forget that doing just that has been the primary focus of our strategy to take these groups down for the past two years?"

Trapp pressed on. "But all that time we've been dealing with ad hoc insurgency groups, not nation state intelligence outfits. By all accounts, the Quds Force guys are professional, even if their professed aims aren't exactly my cup of tea."

"You sure you're on our team, Sergeant?" Breyer remarked acidly.

"Cut it out, gentlemen," Myers said curtly. "We're all on the same side, so let's act like it."

"Sir—"

The captain cut Trapp off. "I'll take your point under advisement, Sergeant. The Air Force has another recon pass scheduled for 1500 hours. If anything's out of place, they'll see it."

Trapp opened his mouth, half-wondering whether he was damaging his career by continuing to hammer the point and deciding he didn't care. "Sir, let me and Sikorski go in ahead of the main attack and get eyes on the village. The drones miss as much as they uncover."

He felt his friend stir beside him at the mention of his name but didn't look around to note the expression on Sikorski's face as he involuntarily volunteered him for the assignment.

Myers paused to consider the suggestion. That was one good thing about Special Operations, Trapp thought. Even in the regular infantry, good officers knew to listen to the expertise of their men. But in SOCOM, it was even more of a two-way street. Myers was rarely on the ground as operations unfolded, whereas Trapp—and every operator in this room—had been on a mission every other night for months. In that time, they'd reached a proficiency with armed combat—and an understanding of their enemy—that few men before them ever had.

"Okay," the captain finally conceded. "You're probably right. You move in at dusk. But whatever you do, don't get caught."

"There's one more thing," Trapp said.

Myers raised his eyebrow. "There always is," he said dryly.

"The kid, Abdel," Trapp replied. "There's an even chance that he's inside the Red Buffalo compound. If he is, that has to affect our Rules of Engagement. We can't go in guns blazing."

"He's not our priority," Breyer interjected curtly. "All I care about is finding those missiles. Until we do that, then a whole lot more kids will be at risk."

Trapp set his jaw. "Then let's make him one."

"Gentlemen," Myers yelled, slapping his palm on the desk

behind him. "Enough! If the boy is there, then we will take all reasonable precautions to bring them out alive. If he's not, it's a moot point. The rest of you, we reassemble here at 1800 hours. Sikorski, Trapp—go get geared up. You'll need to get moving within the hour."

12

"You're awful quiet," Trapp remarked after holding up his fist to signal he needed a drink break. He and Sikorski were crawling down a dried-out irrigation ditch that ran parallel to the border of a field about half a mile from the edge of Ali Daud. The sun had set but had not yet completely disappeared below the horizon. There was just enough natural light to see by, but before long they would be forced to use their night vision.

"Makes a change, huh?" Sikorski replied, reaching for a water canteen that was contained in a soft pouch clipped to his belt to prevent it from bouncing off something hard and giving away their location.

"Makes me think I did something to piss you off," Trapp said, lifting his own canteen to his lips.

"You mean aside from volunteering me for a suicide mission behind enemy lines?" Sikorski quipped before letting out a low chuckle to signal that he was just joking. "Nah. I was just thinking that you were right."

"Now that makes a change," Trapp replied. "But it's about time you recognized my brilliance. About what exactly?"

"Something stinks about this whole operation," Sikorski said. "Everything we know about this Jafari jabroni says he's the kind of man who doesn't make mistakes. I don't know about the dead guy with the tat, Taheri or whatever he was called, but do you think a guy like that would allow amateurs to work with him?"

Trapp answered the rhetorical question. "I do not."

"I figured," Sikorski said dryly. "So that has me wondering what we're all doing here."

"Me too," Trapp said quietly.

A click sounded as Sikorski reattached his canteen to his belt. "Well, I guess we're not going to get the answers we need just lying here. Let's go get eyes on this village. If something's hinky, I guess we're the only ones who can do a damn thing about it."

"Let's hope we're just overthinking things," Trapp said, sensing in his gut that they weren't.

They continued to crawl until they reached the end of the field, where the irrigation ditch disappeared into a length of plastic pipe that was half blocked by stones and debris. They waited there until night fell in earnest to allow them to operate with a little more freedom.

"Hangman, Chopper, how copy?"

"Loud and clear," Trapp murmured, his mind briefly filling with a picture of the man who had given him that nickname. He was also a Ranger, though not currently deployed to the sandbox.

Lucky bastard.

"We have eyes in the sky over your position. You're clear until the village."

Trapp radioed his understanding, then clipped his night vision goggles into place. He extended a closed fist toward Sikorski, who bumped it in return. "Happy hunting," he said.

"Yeah, just so long as we don't end up as the prey."

Both men hoisted themselves out of the ditch and quickly crossed the small border at the edge of the field before stopping in the cover provided by the head-high stalks of Iraqi wheat. They dropped to one knee and scanned in every direction to confirm the information relayed to them from the recon drone above. After five minutes of listening and watching, they glanced at each other and communicated with a silent thumbs-up.

Trapp's heart began beating faster after that, and a familiar gnawing sensation twisted his stomach. There was no substitute for the experience of putting oneself in physical danger and no way it could be explained to those who had not done it. He knew Sikorski felt the same way. It didn't matter how many times they left the wire, each was the same. The day you no longer felt the fear in your belly was probably the one you ate a bullet.

They used the cover provided by the wheat to traverse almost the entire distance that separated them from the village, stopping every fifty yards or so to confirm that they remained undetected. The closer they got, the more frequently they stopped—and the whole while a stream of running updates from the operator of the drone above them buzzed in their ears.

There was only one cardinal instruction for their night's work—to remain unseen. At least until Delta arrived and the shooting began. If it happened before then, the entire operation would be blown.

Trapp's thoughts drifted in the darkness to Nadia's son. He wished he could have given the woman more hope even as he knew that he never could. It wouldn't have been fair. He had promised her everything in his power, which was sparse comfort for either of them. He couldn't stop himself from wondering whether the kid was in there—and if he was, how he was being treated. Surely Omar wasn't so far gone that he would mistreat his own son?

He stifled a cynical snort. It was hardly the first time that such a thing had happened and doubtless wouldn't be the last. Hell, it wasn't even the first time *Omar* had beaten the kid.

As they reached the end of the wheat, he held up a fist and sensed Sikorski tuck in automatically beside him. There was a space of about ten yards between the crops ending and where the village began—in effect an almost unbroken wall of windowless mud walls that marked the rear of each dwelling. The settlement was electrified, though it seemed as though many buildings either didn't have access to the grid or simply couldn't afford to keep the lights running.

Taking a knee, Trapp began to study the village to his left, searching for any signs of life. He took his time, knowing that Sikorski was doing the same to their right. There were endless spaces in which a lookout could be hiding, invisible to the IR cameras in the sky. He glanced at his watch. The gently luminescent hands glowed through goggles that magnified their brightness hundreds of times. It read 1915 hours, leaving over five hours until the assault was scheduled to begin.

"I don't see anything," Sikorski whispered.

"Me neither," Trapp replied a moment later when his scan was complete. "No sentries. Nothing out of the ordinary at all."

"What do you want to do?"

Trapp pointed at a building about five yards to their left. It was a little shorter than many of the other dwellings, and there was an old piece of farm equipment pulled up against it—some kind of geriatric Iraqi tractor that had long since passed into the scrapheap in the sky. "Let's get up on top of that thing. It looks solid."

"You got it," Sikorski agreed.

They moved quickly and silently. It helped that they were traveling light—wearing only essential armor and carrying just their weapons, communications gear, a small amount of ammunition, and little else. When they arrived at the village's outer wall, merely a curious outcome of the way the settlement had developed rather than an intentional defensive structure, they pressed themselves against it as they checked whether they had been spotted.

Trapp had to wait until the blood stopped rushing in his ears before he could listen. Slowly the sounds of the night returned. Just a mile from here was the desert proper, mile after mile of endless, featureless sand. But over countless generations, the local villagers had tapped the River Alwand and used its bounty to create rich, productive agricultural land, which now meant that he heard crickets and the pattering of rodents.

And not much else.

"You hear that?" he whispered.

"What?"

"I'm not sure," Trapp admitted. He couldn't put his finger on what was bugging him, just like in the briefing.

And then he realized. There was no sound of human life. No voices emanating from either televisions or radios, or car engines or children laughing or even their parents hushing them. He checked his watch again just to make sure that he hadn't misread the time.

1921.

Too early for everybody to be in bed, he thought.

"It's too quiet," he said,

"Maybe there ain't much to do here after it gets dark. Not like they're big drinkers out here."

"Yeah," he murmured. "Maybe."

Trapp reached out and tested the old tractor, pushing down hard until he was certain the rusted machine wouldn't squeal when he put his full weight on it. Sikorski did the same when he was done.

"Just checking your work," he said with a grin.

"You go first," Trapp said. "I'll cover."

Sikorski nodded his understanding, then slung his rifle over his back and make sure that it was both secure and wouldn't shift as he climbed. Trapp shot him a thumbs-up.

Once he was on the tractor, the Ranger was tall enough to reach the roof of the building. It was only a single story. He reached up with his right, then left hand and fastened each on the edge of the wall, moving slowly and carefully and making sure that his grip was solid before he continued. Trapp left one eye on him, but most of the rest of his attention was occupied with making sure there were no threats to their rear.

Next, Sikorski lifted his right leg and nestled his boot into a slight crack in the wall. A little dust coursed to the ground as he made sure that his foothold was secure, but it did so noiselessly. There seemed little danger of dislodging a larger, louder chunk of debris from the solid structure.

Finally, the lithe operator hoisted himself up and over the lip of the wall in almost total silence, driving with his right foot the same time as he pulled upward with all the strength in his arms and back. He disappeared out of Trapp's sight, leaving only darkness where he'd just been.

"Clear," came an almost inaudible call about thirty seconds later. "I've got you."

Trapp followed the route that Sikorski had picked out a moment before and joined his friend on the roof without breaking a sweat. He was greeted with a pat on the shoulder as he lay flat on his belly. The day's heat rose back off the surface and warmed his chest.

"Man, this place is dead," Sikorski whispered. "Looks half-abandoned."

He wasn't wrong. If Ali Daud had ever been a prosperous place, it certainly wasn't any longer. The building Trapp and Sikorski were lying on had once hosted a television antenna, but the device had long since rusted into obsolescence. The cable that had carried Saddam's propaganda broadcasts into the dwelling below was frayed and snapped.

The roof was low, but then so was the rest of the village. It provided enough of a vantage point to see about thirty yards of the road that Delta's Fox element was supposed to take before hitting the Red Buffalo compound, right up until the road kinked to the left and led to the building.

Trapp dropped his eye to his rifle's thermal scope. The street immediately lit up in grays and whites, outlining spots where the heat of the day was now radiating back out of the ground. An ancient-looking sedan parked at about the midpoint of the street was warmest of all and glowed brightly in the gloom. He swept the weapon to the right but saw nothing else before the road hooked back around, then did the same to the left.

He stopped as the sweep revealed something that had been invisible to the naked eye. A man was seated underneath the awning of what might have been a shop as far to the left as he could see, about fifteen yards before the parked car. An object glowed in his right hand, and Trapp watched as the man lifted it to his lips and took a drag from his cigarette.

"At least someone's awake," he whispered, gesturing toward the target so that Sikorski could take a look.

"It's not such a bad life," his partner agreed. "I don't see a weapon."

"Me neither."

Trapp crawled to the edge of the roof, pausing right before he made it to ensure that his gear was tightly secured to his frame, then looked over. The building he was lying on was little more than a shell. There was no door, and it was entirely dark inside. He looked right and saw that the next five houses looked the same: all dark, though less obviously abandoned than this one. It was the same to the left. Perhaps seven empty buildings, then one or two out of which a little electric light leaked out through shuttered windows and from underneath doors.

He pushed himself back and slowly rose into a kneeling

position, looking out across the tops of the buildings that stretched all the way to the northeast edge of the village, the farthest point away from the river. Most lights gleamed around the edge of the settlement, as though it was prime real estate, though he couldn't figure why. The center resembled the inky blackness of a satellite shot of North Korea taken at night.

"Sergeant Trapp, how copy?"

Immediately recognizing Captain Myers's voice over the radio net, Trapp backed away from the edge of the roof. He spoke in a hushed tone. "I read you, Captain."

"Give me a status report."

"Sir, we just arrived in position. The target looks quiet. So far, no evidence of either armed insurgents or military age males, but it seems like everybody's tucked up inside. If anyone's here at all."

"Any sign of trouble?"

"Not so far. But something smells off about this, Captain. I'm not exactly sure what it is, but this place gives me the willies."

"You have anything more concrete than the willies?"

"No, sir."

"Okay, stay put. Radio in if you see anything concerning."

Trapp grimaced. "Copy, sir. Permission to recon farther into the village?"

Myers paused for a second before responding. "Negative. Too risky. Hold tight where you are."

"Sir—"

"I backed your play, Trapp, and you got me the information I needed. Now your work is done. Myers out."

Trapp formed a fist and ground it into his thigh, frustrated to have been denied. With the recon drone operating somewhere over his head, it wasn't even as if he could interpret his orders creatively and go for a little look-see without being spotted.

"I guess we better make ourselves comfortable," Sikorski said, looking equally disappointed. "It's 1930. We've got a long time to wait."

Eyeing his rifle's scope once again, Trapp focused in on the man smoking at the far end of the street. He seemed completely relaxed, as though he did this every night.

"You see that guy?" he said.

"Sure. Same as he was before."

"Right. You see anything weird about the building he's sitting in front of?"

Sikorski shook his head. "No. Oh…"

"Yeah," Trapp whispered. "No lights. That's weird, right?"

"Feels that way," Sikorski agreed. "But it doesn't really mean shit, does it? Maybe he's late on his bills."

Trapp lowered himself backward into a seated position, then rolled back onto his front to shrink his profile. Sikorski rolled his neck slowly. They were far enough from the edge of the flat roof that nobody would be able to spot them from the ground. Without night vision, it was unlikely anyone on a nearby roof would be able to either.

"Nope," he muttered.

He couldn't help but feel that there were forces at work here that he did not fully understand. Finding that first empty missile crate had led them to Omar's farm. Nadia had led them to Burnt Ridge, where the narrowly averted disaster had built an inexorable pressure on Captain Myers and Colonel Ruzzier to get results and put an end to the missile threat—and quickly.

And that had led him and Sikorski to Ali Daud. Soon, many more Americans would come to this place.

It was as though they were all just pawns on a chessboard, and some unseen hand was slowly, methodically moving his pieces into position.

But to what end?

13

"Checkpoint Alpha," a terse voice stated simply over the radio net, signaling that the Echo and Fox detachments had left the main highway. The two sniper teams had worked their way into position about half an hour earlier and had reported clear fields of fire on the target compound.

Still nothing stirred in the village. It was so quiet that Trapp began to believe he'd talked himself into an unwarranted state of anxiety. The operation would proceed smoothly after all. Delta would knock down a door, snatch a bad guy out of bed, wrap a kid up in cotton wool, and it would all be over in minutes.

The smoker had retreated inside for about an hour but was now back on his doorstep, steadily chaining his way through what had to be a second pack of cigarettes. Trapp guided his rifle's scope back in the man's direction, fixing it in place and studying the subject intently for anything he'd missed.

"Fox, checkpoint Bravo," another voice reported. This signal meant that the two Delta detachments had separated where the road forked into two lanes to enter the village.

Trapp's heart beat faster. This thing was happening, whether he liked it or not.

"You good?" he whispered at Sikorski.

"Yeah." His friend nodded grimly.

"Me neither." Trapp grinned back.

"Echo, checkpoint Charlie."

Trapp could hear the vehicles now. They were moving fast but not recklessly. Probably forty kilometers an hour—about as quickly as the Austrian-built armored vehicles could go in a built-up environment without risking an accident. The smoker didn't seem to care. Finally he swept his scope away from the man. In thirty seconds' time, his concerns would be academic. That was about how long it would take for the two Delta elements to make it to Red Buffalo.

"Our friend just stood up," Sikorski muttered.

Panning back, Trapp saw that he was right. The smoker dropped his present cigarette—lit only a few seconds earlier—and crushed it underneath his boot before disappearing back inside his shop. Trapp's stomach knotted with tension, his gut screaming that something was wrong with this picture.

But still Myers's words echoed in his skull. He didn't have anything concrete. And interrupting the strike element now might be as dangerous as letting them proceed into an ambush. Speed was critical, and doubt was like friction, slowing everything it touched.

The first of Fox's armored vehicles skidded around the corner and became visible at the edge of Trapp's vision. The grumble of its engine was unmistakable. It was traveling without lights, but the heat from the engine glowed through his scope. It ate up the yards rapidly and reached the sedan halfway up the street in the blink of an eye.

The car detonated with sufficient force to throw both Trapp and Sikorski physically back, almost to the far edge of the building's roof. Trapp's helmet smashed backward and bounced off the structure, rattling his brains as a flash of light burned his vision. His throat wheezed as he sucked in desperately needed oxygen, though the air seemed thinner, as though the explosion had consumed it all. His mind was clogged, but he knew he needed to act. Men's lives were at risk. He just didn't what he was supposed to do.

Finally, he remembered. He grabbed his radio and brought it to his lips.

"Ambush!" he screamed into the transmitter, barely hearing his own voice over the ringing in his ears and the pops of secondary explosions in the street in front of him. "Echo, bug the hell out, now!"

It was too late. A second brilliant yellow cloud of flame erupted fifty yards away on the other side of the village. Echo must have hit an identical IED. This trap had been meticulously prepared.

Trapp dragged himself to the edge of the roof. A chunk had broken away from the front from the force of the explosion, leaving a toothy gap. If anyone was on the radio net, he couldn't hear them. He could see the flames burning in front of him, but they did so silently—at least it seemed that way.

He was seeing double. He shook his head to try and clear it, but the issue persisted. His chest ached from the force of the pressure wave, and his hearing rang incessantly. He squeezed his eyes shut, and as he did so, he felt something hard coming down on his back. He rolled over and stared up, reaching for his weapon as his brain signaled a threat—but saw Sikorski instead. His fist was raised.

His friend's features finally resolved at the same moment as the ringing died away and the sound of the world returned. Flames hissed on the street below, as well as something altogether more concerning.

Gunfire.

"They're fucking everywhere!" Sikorski yelled, pointing out at the village. Blood was trickling out of his left ear.

Trapp stared up at him absently. His chest heaved, and his head slowly began to drop back as though it weighed down a hundred pounds. It would be so easy to fall asleep, to give in to what his body wanted.

No.

He forced himself to resist. He could hear the gunshots now and the occasional whoomph that he instantly placed as an RPG detonating. He rolled back onto his front, then pushed himself up into a kneeling position, bringing his rifle to his shoulder.

For a moment, he just stared open-mouthed at the chaos. The quiet little village of Ali Daud had turned into a war zone. In the street below, the first of the two Pandur armored vehicles had rolled onto its side. Smoke poured out of the upper wheel well, and flames licked its scarred armor. It was instantly clear that this was the most intense battle he'd ever experienced, and it was only just getting warmed up.

The second Pandur hadn't fared much better. It had escaped the worst of the damage inflicted by the detonation of the car bomb, only to hit a mine buried in the road. A crater was now gouged into the earth where it had been laid. Like the first, this Pandur wasn't going anywhere fast.

There was worse news to come. At least a dozen insurgents had appeared from seemingly nowhere—Trapp now under-stood the meaning of all those darkened buildings—and were raining small arms fire down onto the crippled vehicles.

"Fox," Trapp called urgently into his radio as Sikorski began calmly and methodically engaging targets. "Anybody alive in there?"

"Barely," a pained voice replied after a short delay. "But we're all breathing. It's a mobility kill for sure, but these things are tough cookies."

Trapp broke away from the conversation for a moment as he caught a glimpse of an insurgent armed with a rocket-propelled grenade popping up out of a trap door onto the roof on the opposite side of the street. He brought his rifle up, closed his left eye, and dropped the target. Even as he did so, he watched as another pair of fighters maneuvered a machine gun into position and started pounding the smoking lead Pandur.

"I suggest you remain in there for the time being. It's pretty fucking toasty out here."

As the second armored vehicle radioed that they too were in one piece, the insurgents finally seemed to realize they had company. Rounds began impacting the roof upon which Trapp and Sikorski lay, driving them back.

"Fox, this is Golf. We do not have a firing solution from our current location. Correcting now," the sniper pair reported. "We'll be out of the fight for at least two minutes."

"Fox copies," came the reply. Disconcertingly, Trapp could hear the metallic clang of rounds impacting the Pandur's armor from inside the vehicle through the radio. "This thing will hold out against small arms fire until Judgment Day. But if those assholes are packing anything heavier, we'll be sitting ducks."

Trapp had worked that much out for himself. He and Sikorski traded positions laying down covering fire, one shooting as the other reloaded. But at the rate they were burning through their limited ammunition—traveling light no longer seemed like such a good idea—they wouldn't be able to keep up for long.

"If we stay here, we're screwed," he shouted at Sikorski. "And so are they."

Through the radio, he could hear Echo and Hotel communicating. Echo seemed to have come off a little lighter from the initial ambush but was nonetheless under sustained pressure from another group of insurgents. Worse still, the Ranger units on the river were also coming under fire from entrenched machine gun nests. They'd been forced to pull back and would have to approach the village on foot.

But that would take time they didn't have.

"Concur," Sikorski replied succinctly. He jerked his chin at the machine gun position across the street. "You think we can take that out of action before we go?"

Trapp checked his own ammunition supply. Three mags left. It wasn't enough. "I've got a better idea," he said. "Let's capture it."

Groaning, Sikorski yelled, "I had a bad feeling you were going to say that."

A storm of gunfire gouged chunks of debris out of the rooftop and kicked it up into Trapp's face. It was a miracle that neither of them had yet been hit. Clouds of dust and smoke from the ambush below made it difficult to see, let alone shoot accurately. The only blessing was that the same issue afflicted the men firing at them.

"We need to move," Trapp said. "You go first. I'll cover."

He fired another half dozen rounds, then indicated a building two units farther down the street. It had a lip on the edge of its roof that was about a foot and a half tall—barely enough to shield them but better than nothing. It would be easy enough to traverse the adjacent flat roofs to reach it—at least if people weren't shooting back.

He unclipped a grenade from his plate carrier, wishing he'd been foresighted enough to pack more. "Frag out!"

Sikorski didn't wait a second after it detonated before he sprinted to the adjacent rooftop. Trapp kneeled, firing three-round bursts into the chaos to conserve his ammunition as he covered his friend.

"I deserve," Sikorski called out, huffing and grunting from the effort of his brush with death as he huddled behind the meager shelter provided by the lip on the edge of the new roof, "a fucking long vacation. Somewhere real cold. I'm sick of this goddamn heat. And the bullets. Especially the fucking bullets."

"Yeah? Then you probably shouldn't have joined the Army," Trapp fired back.

Sikorski wiped the sweat off his brow. "Wise guy. You ready?"

"As I'll ever be."

Sikorski flashed him a thumbs-up, crossed himself, and rose into the maelstrom. As soon as the Ranger's gun began to crackle, Trapp made the same journey, sprinting as chips of mortar broke off the roof beneath him and tore at his fatigues. Bullets snapped unseen through the smoke, portents of death that would have pushed most rational minds into retreat.

But retreat meant death too. Just slower and more drawn out. There was only one way out of this fight: to take it to the enemy—and to defeat them.

But with Fox's commandos pinned inside their armored vehicles, Echo taking heavy fire on the other side of the village, a crippling absence of air cover, and the Rangers on the river forced to fall back before they could push forward, Trapp, Sikorski, and a few snipers were all that was left to hold the line.

All this went through Trapp's mind as he threw himself to the ground next to Sikorski. On the other side of the street, several of the insurgents seemed to have identified their new position and were laying down consistent—if haphazardly aimed—fire.

"You made it," Sikorski said, ducking down beside him.

"By the skin of my teeth," Trapp hissed, sucking in air that was thick with smoke. "You couldn't do something about those assholes?"

"Unfortunately, that comes with the gold package, and you only plumped for silver. Nothing I can do about it. It's policy."

"I thought the customer was never wrong."

Sikorski shrugged, though the strained expression on his

face indicated that there were limits to even his famously light nature. "You haven't paid yet."

Trapp's earpiece crackled. "Fox, this is Golf. We are in position. Holding fire until we hear from you."

"Finally some good news," Trapp muttered. "How much ammunition you got?"

"Two mags," Sikorski replied without needing to look. "Maybe half a dozen more rounds in the rifle. And a couple of mags for the Glock, but if it gets that desperate—"

"We may as well throw the damn things at the bastards." Trapp grinned.

"Something like that."

"I'm about the same," Trapp said. He pushed the radio transmit button. "Golf, this is Hangman. Do you have eyes on the street?"

"We wouldn't be much use if we didn't, Hangman," Golf replied coolly.

Sikorski chuckled, barely flinching as a round impacted the roof only a few inches away from his head, sending a shower of chips and dust rattling down against his helmet. "You gotta admit, that was a dumb question."

Ignoring the gibe, Trapp continued, "How many tangos are we looking at?"

"Maybe twelve? That's not a comprehensive count. I see at least six on the rooftops—two manning that machine gun nest, the rest mostly equipped with small arms—"

An explosion in the street below prompted a fresh radio transmission from Fox. "And RPGs. That one near enough scrambled my brain. Maybe you guys can leave the catch-up till later?"

Golf continued as though he hadn't even noticed the interruption.

"—And the rest are inside the buildings on either side of

the street. Looks like they hollowed out the interior walls. Smart."

"Okay," Trapp replied, thinking fast. "You think you can pin down the guys on the roof on my mark? We're running out of ammo up here, but if we can reach that MG nest, we should be able to mop up the fighters inside the buildings and get some more of our guys into the fight."

"You got it."

Sikorski reached over and tapped Trapp's shoulder, then pointed to the next roof over. "You see it?"

Trapp squinted as he tried to make out what his friend was referring to. A fresh cloud smoke poured out of the street below, momentarily obscuring his sight completely. It was only when it cleared that he finally saw it: a trap door leading into the building below.

"Oh, that's *definitely* going to be locked from the inside," he said.

"Well, since between us you're definitely the strongest, I volunteer you to try and break through," Sikorski said.

"You've changed your tune," Trapp griped good-naturedly. "Cover me?"

"Figure it's the least I could do."

"When we get in, head straight for the ground floor," Trapp said, taking it as given that he would make it through the door and not die in the attempt. "We don't know for sure how many tangos there are down there. If we get into a fight with them, all we'll do is let them know we're here."

"Yeah, you got it," Sikorski said, shooting him an A-OK sign. "Let's just cross the roof of death, drop in on a bunch of amped-up Iraqi insurgents without them catching on, then cross a street that's being fired on from both sides—without anybody noticing. *Again*."

"You got a grenade?" Trapp asked, sidestepping his friend's grumbling.

"One left," Sikorski said, unclipping it and handing it over. "Don't use it all at once."

"I make no promises," Trapp replied, hefting the explosive in his right palm and closing one eye as he measured the distance to the trapdoor.

"You are not thinking what I think you're thinking, are you?"

"Thankfully, Sikorski, I'm not in that filthy head of yours," he replied before switching to his radio. "Golf, pin them down, would you?"

After that, Trapp blocked the world out. He guessed it was about ten yards to the trapdoor, which was a recessed square not much wider than the span of his shoulders in both directions. Except for a few chunks of debris, the roof was entirely flat. He took a steadying breath, pulled the pin, and tossed the grenade in a flat arc.

"Frag out," he called.

It bounced off the opposite roof, then skittered along its surface before falling into the hole that housed the trapdoor. After a pause of about two seconds, it detonated in a spout of dust and shrapnel.

"Sorry I doubted you," Sikorski muttered, sounding impressed.

A fresh sound of gunfire entered the fray—this time louder, single shots, spaced a couple of seconds apart. Golf had started mopping up the insurgents on top of the buildings on the opposite side of the street. The volume of suppressing fire heading their way dropped immediately.

"Let's go." Trapp sprinted toward the next roof over without waiting for acknowledgment. The grenade had damaged the entrance into the building below without completely destroying it. He reversed his rifle in his hands and smashed its stock down repeatedly in clean, powerful blows, sweeping the remnants of the wood away like glass fragments in a broken window frame.

When he was finished, Sikorski lowered the barrel of his rifle into the room below and pumped half a dozen rounds into the darkness.

"I'll take point," he said before dropping his legs through the hole and lowering himself inside. He held on for a second before falling gracefully to the floor.

Trapp held his breath, but since no further flashes of muzzle fire erupted down below, he figured the room had to be empty.

"You coming, partner?" Sikorski inquired in a low voice.

He followed him inside. The room was pitch black, though Sikorski had already clicked on the IR flashlight on the barrel of his rifle. Trapp did the same. The sounds of the battle outside were more muffled now through the thick concrete walls. As far as either of them could tell, there were no insurgents inside this particular building.

They made it downstairs without encountering trouble. As Golf had intimated, holes had been created between individual homes along the street. They were easily wide enough to allow a man to pass through, even loaded down with weapons. It would've taken hours to penetrate and widen the gaps in each thick wall, and he noticed no tools more sophisticated than a sledgehammer.

"They must've planned this for weeks," he whispered to Sikorski. "Maybe longer."

"No kidding," came the equally hushed reply.

"I figure most of the bad guys will be upstairs," Trapp continued. "Easier to cover the ambush site that way. Let's turn their rat run against them. We need to get as far down the street as possible so that we don't cross in the middle of a gunfight."

Sikorski nodded. He crouched by the hole in the wall and

looked through, using his rifle's IR beam to provide illumination. "Clear."

They scrambled through half a dozen buildings like ghosts. Occasionally they heard gunfire or the sound of voices from the floors above, but they saw no one.

"That's far enough," Trapp said, his heart pounding from the effort. "You ready?"

Sikorski nodded.

"Golf, this is Hangman. Request suppressing fire, we're about to make our dash."

"Copy, Hangman," came the Delta operator's cool, unruffled voice. "On your mark."

Trapp and Sikorski readied themselves by the home's front door. As they passed through the building, they saw evidence that a family lived here. Kids' toys, pans on hooks on the wall. They must've moved out in a hurry.

"Mark."

14

Trapp sprinted across the devastated street, crossing it in a matter of seconds with Sikorski close behind. Without Golf providing suppressing fire, it would have been a trivial matter for the insurgents dug into reinforced fighting positions to chew them up. As it was, the sniper and shooter team bought valuable breathing space.

He snapped a mental picture of the battlefield as he ran. The troop hatches of both the upright and the crippled Pandur fighting vehicles were angled slightly away from the side of the street on which he'd just arrived. This left them fully exposed to incoming fire from the other side, but if he and Sikorski could only make it to the machine gun, they would be able to put down sufficient fire for the Delta commandos to free themselves and join the fight without being wiped out.

"You okay?" Sikorski asked, wheezing like he smoked twenty a day after inhaling a lungful of whatever toxic chemicals were coming off the smoldering troop vehicles.

"Never better," Trapp said, pressing himself against the wall. He mopped thick, dusty rivulets of sweat from his forehead, wincing as the salty, filthy liquid stung his eyes. They were now about thirty yards farther up the street from the building they'd scaled at the start of all this. It seemed that the insurgents hadn't yet cottoned on to what they were up to. "Ready?"

"Yep," came the reply after Sikorski hiked up a full mouthful of spit and disposed of it, a distasteful snarl on his face. The sight of him now gave the lie to his demeanor. He was more than a soldier with a sense of humor. He was a killer.

Trapp led, keeping his frame pressed up tight against the wall to his left. He entered the first home he came across, which —like the rest of them—was empty. The first room he entered was a kitchen of sorts, containing a stove that was no more than a couple of burners attached to a freestanding gas bottle. The place had been packed up neatly, reinforcing Trapp's suspicion that this ambush had been a long time coming. Somebody had told these people to get out. Probably taken them somewhere safe to ensure they kept their mouth shut until the operation was over. It had happened long enough ago for the insurgents to pry a hole through the wall here too.

Another RPG detonated in the street, sending shrapnel and debris flying. There would be time to figure it all out after.

"Clear," he said in a low whisper. "From here on out we go dark, okay?"

Sikorski nodded his understanding.

"Hangman, this is Golf. That machine gun nest has us pinned. They're switching fire between us and the fighting vehicles. We won't be much use to you from here on out."

"Understood. Working on it."

Trapp flashed the index and middle finger on his left hand, indicating it was time to move. As Sikorski had done on the other side of the street, he crouched and used his IR flashlight to check the room on the other side. It was clear. But this time, they would have to fight their way up. That was a whole different ball game.

He crawled through, taking a knee to cover the room until Sikorski joined him. They repeated the maneuver several times, each time entering empty houses. But the farther they crawled, the louder the noise of battle grew.

"Here," Trapp breathed, pointing at a brick stairwell in the corner of the room. He judged they'd made it far enough across. The machine gun was either situated on top of this building or on one to either side. It was difficult to be certain. One thing was for sure, though. There were men upstairs.

Armed men.

Again, Sikorski signaled his readiness. Both men switched out their half-spent magazines for fresh ones, storing the one they'd ejected, just in case. Trapp crept toward the stairwell, keeping his frame low. He hoped that the fighters upstairs would be so consumed by adrenaline and the fury of battle that he and Sikorski would be able to sneak up on them.

There was nothing honorable about shooting a man in the back. But it was a hell of a lot easier than waiting until he turned around and started firing back.

Footsteps thundered down the stairs. A white glow exploded in Trapp's night vision. As a man rounded the corner down the stairs, both he and Sikorski squeezed their triggers in unison. The insurgent dropped dead, a flashlight falling from his left hand and tumbling down the stairs, an AK-pattern rifle from his right.

"Fuck."

The element of surprise was well and truly gone.

But they still had a job to do. Trapp advanced, stamping down hard on the flashlight and hearing a satisfying crunch as the cheap plastic casing shattered underneath his heavy boot. Once again, the space was flooded with a darkness through which only he and Sikorski could see. Their night vision was effectively a superpower. Ordinarily, it made firefights against opponents who were not similarly equipped akin to shooting fish in a barrel. Tonight, given the enemy's overwhelming numerical superiority, it just evened up the odds.

He bent and picked up the Kalashnikov from the dead insurgent's hands, draping the strap over his left shoulder. The way his ammo supplies were going, he might need it sooner than he liked.

"Leading," he called and advanced up the stairs. They kinked to the left at exactly the point the Iraqi had appeared from. Trapp pivoted the same way as he reached the large, square step at the center of the stairwell. Muzzle flashes lit up the room above in staccato cracks of sound and light. There was more than one shooter.

Trapp didn't stop to count. He surged up the stairwell, entering the room and dropping the first of three insurgents in the same movement as one of them fired into the street while two conferred—perhaps over what the hell had happened to their friend downstairs. That pair reacted quicker than their unlucky associate, diving for cover behind a haphazard assortment of furniture.

"Covering," Sikorski said loudly, seemingly reading Trapp's mind. The Ranger depressed his trigger, firing clipped bursts with barely a second between them to fix both insurgents in position. Trapp counted the shots in his mind, waiting for his moment to strike. A full magazine, minus three rounds fired at the guy on the stairs.

Now.

He moved before Sikorski's weapon ran dry, vaulting over the couch in the center of the room and squeezing his trigger as he came down on the other side. He killed one of the insurgents at point blank range, delivering a brutal kick to the midriff of the other the second his feet were anywhere near stable. The man collapsed, dropping his weapon in the process. Trapp drew his own rifle back, ready to fire, but caught himself. He kicked the unlucky Iraqi a second time, ensuring he was down for the count, then dropped to one knee and bound the man's wrists behind his back with a pair of flex cuffs from a pouch on his plate carrier. They were a standard, essential part of his load out.

"Hey, didn't know I was shipping out with Jackie Chan," Sikorski whistled.

"There's a lot you don't know about me," Trapp replied grimly. He felt the shakes starting to come on, the inevitable consequence of mainlining on adrenaline for longer than the body could sustain the quick fix of energy. But he didn't have a choice. He kicked the weapons away from the dead men on the floor out of habit, grabbing a couple of spare magazines for his borrowed rifle as he did so.

"Clear," Sikorski said, checking the rathole to the building on the left as Trapp did the same on the right. "I don't see any fighters for a couple buildings. They probably have no idea what just went down. Not with all this noise."

"Same here," Trapp said, looking up in search for a way onto the roof. "Can we get up–? *There.*"

"I don't see any grenades," Sikorski said in a disappointed tone as he crouched down to rustle through a couple of boxes of weapons and ammunition the dead insurgents had left behind.

"Then let's hope no one's waiting for us up there," Trapp replied as he cased the route to the roof.

"I'll take point," Sikorski said, moving toward the ladder that his friend had just spotted. He let his rifle fall against the single-point sling on his plate carrier, drawing the pistol holstered at his waist instead. He experimentally placed a boot on the ladder's first rung, and once satisfied the aged wood wasn't going to snap, he began to climb.

He led with the pistol before poking his head into the night sky with an abundance of caution, moving inch by inch as Trapp made sure that nobody was coming up behind.

Desperate calls on the radio came from both Fox on the street below and Echo—who it appeared had at least made it out of their armored vehicles before coming under fire. They had injured men but were fighting a professional rearguard action.

Sikorski beckoned him up, placing two fingers over his lips and motioning for silence. Trapp nodded and began to climb. Once his head was free of the opening onto the roof, he passed the AK through and quietly set it down so that it didn't clatter against anything as he hauled his bulk the rest of the way.

As he emerged onto the roof, the heavy thump of the machine gun became audible. It was resting on a tripod and firing northeast down the street, tracer rounds reaching out and bouncing off the tallest of the squat, featureless dwellings inside. Its target had to be where the Delta snipers had set up.

"Any time now would be great," Golf radioed, stress finally breaking through his heretofore studied manner.

The two gunners operating the weapon were completely engrossed in their task, probably half deafened from the continuous firing from the heavy gun, whose muzzle flashes lit up the night sky. The surface of the roof was covered in brass shell casings, with barely an inch of dried mud still visible. Trapp and Sikorski communicated using hand signals, identifying a target each. Both men aimed, then fired.

The heavy gun fell silent.

Though the fight was far from over, Trapp clenched his fist. He took no satisfaction at the death of other men, but when they were shooting at his friends, he had no other choice. He scrambled to the adjacent roof, lifting the gun up and raising it over the edge before aiming down.

"Fox, this is Hangman," he panted as Sikorski wrestled to slap a fresh ammunition belt into place. "You get to skip detention in about ten seconds. Get ready."

Beneath him, muzzle flashes spat fire into the night from both sides of the street. It was difficult to pick out who was who in the chaos. But Trapp carefully picked out a nest of the enemy and squeezed the machine gun's trigger. The weapon's rate of fire far outpaced anything else the insurgents had in their locker. In a matter of seconds, bullet holes pockmarked the street's façade, punching through the mud walls and making the already scarred surface resemble nothing more than the face of the moon. The gunfire from that side of the street diminished instantly as the militants dived for cover.

"We're ready, Hangman," Fox replied. "We'll move on your command."

Trapp kept shooting, squeezing the trigger in steady bursts as he moved his aim across each of the first-floor buildings on the opposite side of the street in turn. It didn't take long. By the time the ammo belt ran dry, there was nobody left to shoot.

He sank backward, letting the stock of the machine gun thud against the roof as a wave of sudden exhaustion washed over him.

"Fox, you're clear to exit," Sikorski radioed. "Still a few tangos on our side of the street. Mop them up for us, would you?"

"Our pleasure."

Fresh crackles of gunfire echoed in the street below as the Delta commandos exited their still smoldering vehicles. They fired in smooth, calm bursts, quickly but methodically wiping out all opposition. In thirty seconds, it was over.

Sikorski reached over with clenched fist and bumped it against Trapp's shoulder. "That was a hell of a close shave," he said, shaking his head. "Could've been a whole lot of us going back home wrapped in flags."

Trapp simply nodded mutely. With the adrenaline fading from his system, he could barely muster the energy to think, let alone speak. He should've felt elated, but instead, an emptiness had its claws in him.

A new voice burst onto the radio net. "Fox, this is Echo. We got a real bad problem here. Lewis is KIA, and Breyer's gone."

"What do you mean gone?" one of Fox's commandos radioed.

"Missing. Lewis took a bullet to the face, and as we were trying to save him, a whole phalanx of tangos converged on us. They knew what they were doing. It was like they had the whole thing planned."

"Moving to your position now, Echo," the Delta operator transmitted.

Sikorski looked at Trapp, for once too stunned to speak. A wave of nausea rose from Trapp's gut as the last few pieces of the puzzle finally fell into place. This had never just been about an ambush or killing a few American grunts to add to the body count read out on the nightly news.

Jafari had wanted this all along. He'd planned every step meticulously. Made sure it was Task Force Center who came after him, then taken away their key advantage: air mobility. Tempted them into a trap, then closed its jaws the second they were inside.

But to what end? There were checkpoints on every road out of the village. A drone was circling in the sky overhead. Even if they had Breyer, they couldn't get him out.

Trapp's eyes went wide as he figured it out. "Oh, shit."

15

A punishing sequence of detonations echoed from the opposite side of Ali Daud, and shortly after the tempo of radio messages from the beleaguered Delta commandos increased noticeably. Just judging by the sound of the battle, Trapp figured that the insurgents had concentrated most of their forces at Echo's ambush site, leaving a smaller detachment in his present location as a delaying force.

"What?" Sikorski said. Judging by the look on his face, he was repeating the question. Maybe not for the first time. "What is it?"

"I think I know how they plan to get out," Trapp replied, kneeling to scoop up a fresh mag for his borrowed AK. "Grab as much ammo as you can. This could get messy."

Sikorski got to work, stripping a rifle from the body of one of the gunners and searching the man's frame for additional magazines. He found four, one of which he tossed in Trapp's direction. "You care to share your deductions, Sherlock? Because there's a whole lot of us here who would like to know."

"I'm not certain," Trapp admitted. "It's a long shot, but I

don't see they have any other way to get Breyer out of the village. You with me?"

"To the grave," Sikorski said, before adding, "but hopefully not that far. What are you thinking?"

"Whoever planned this—Jafari, whoever—they've been a step ahead of us this whole time," Trapp said, frisking the other corpse for mags to add to those he'd already liberated. He stuffed them into the webbing on his plate carrier but kept his H&K clipped to the front of it to use as his primary weapon until it ran dry.

"No kidding," Sikorski said, squatting on his haunches and staring out at the battlefield that had consumed the quiet village of Ali Daud. The glow of flame colored the clouds in the night sky a dull ochre, and every few seconds, the detonation of an RPG rocked the settlement, punctuating the incessant but more muted rattle of gunfire.

"He wanted us to come here in the first place. Let's assume his ultimate goal was to kill as many of us as possible—and ideally capture one if an opportunity presented itself. Then he needed an exfil route. But a guy that smart would've known we would have the roads blocked off, as well as a security screen a mile or so out."

"Then what? You think he's got a helicopter on the way?" Sikorski said. His face lit up as he found a fresh grenade.

"Doubtful. We might not be able to bring any of our own choppers in, but an F-16 out of Anaconda could be here in twenty minutes. No point going to all that effort just to get blown out of the sky."

"We might not shoot it down if Breyer was inside."

"I think he planned something better."

Sikorski simply raised an eyebrow.

"The river," Trapp said.

"Our guys have it interdicted," Sikorski said, before echoing

Trapp's refrain from a little earlier as he worked out that the Ranger boats had been forced to pull back. "Oh, crap."

"My thoughts exactly," Trapp said, standing upright now that he was finished stripping the body of the dead insurgent.

Both men listened as a radio transmission came through their headsets. "Echo, this is Fox. We've mopped up here. Moving to your position to assist. Fox out."

"Do we go with them?" Sikorski asked.

"No, you and I head for the river," Trapp said. "I might be way off."

Sikorski made for the access hatch on the building's roof, but Trapp shook his head. He gestured at the expense of flat roofs that ran in an almost direct line to the river. "There's a quicker way."

The two men pounded the hard roofs, their weapons clanking against each other. The AK slung over Trapp's left shoulder kept bouncing against his hipbone, hard enough that he suspected the skin would be bruised black and blue in the morning.

"Command, this is Hangman. Do you have eyes on the river? May be a possible exfil route for the hostage."

"Vectoring now, Hangman," came the reply.

Trapp couldn't hear the sound of the Predator's engines over the din of battle. But it was impossible to miss the dual streaks of light, flame and smoke that exploded from opposite sides of the village.

There were missiles here, after all.

For a moment, both he and Sikorski halted their headlong sprint and stared helplessly up into the sky. The surface-to-air missiles rose on columns of light and smoke as their bright engines rocketed upward. There was a delay of about four seconds, then a display as impressive as any New Year's fireworks erupted above them.

"Dammit," Trapp said, his tongue drive from dust and smoke and almost numb with shock.

"All units, be advised we no longer have ISR coverage overhead," a radio operator's voice from the mission's command post reported. "We're working on it."

"No shit," Sikorski muttered, his chin dropping slowly to parallel as he watched the drone's flaming debris tumble toward the ground laced with rivulets of trailing smoke. Smaller detonations cooked off in the sky above as pockets of fuel in tanks and other components exploded, causing smaller pieces of detritus to spark off like flares in the night.

"Guess it's just us, then."

"Command, this is Hangman. Moving to get eyes on the river now. Over."

"Understood, Hangman. Be advised, we cannot spare any additional units at this time."

"Did Bravo leave anyone guarding the boats?"

"Negative, Hangman. All Ranger units are inbound on foot."

"Great," Trapp muttered without transmitting, rearranging the rifle on his left shoulder and beginning to jog once more. He vaulted a gap between two buildings and started building up speed.

He transmitted as he ran. "Get at least one squad back to the boats. If that's how they are planning on getting Breyer out, then we need to be able to follow them."

"Concur, Hangman. Working on it."

As a new stream of commands was issued over the radio net, he and Sikorski blocked out the noise. The good news was that nobody was shooting at them. The bad news was that they'd just reached the end of the road.

Or at least the roof.

"Ah man, this is going to hurt," Sikorski muttered, eyeing the jump from the top of the building they were presently standing on into the walled compound below. There was a small brick outhouse about three feet away from the building's outer wall. It was only about five foot high, which meant a drop of at least twelve feet.

"If you wanted to be able to walk after your 40th birthday, you shouldn't have joined the 75th." Trapp shrugged. He took a step back, focusing on the roof of the outhouse and visualizing the jump in his mind. He drew his right hand back, palm flat as a blade and pictured it punching forward as he threw his bulk into the air.

"In all fairness, that wasn't what the recruiter promised me," Sikorski replied.

"That was your first mistake."

Trapp's stomach lurched from underneath him as he hurled himself through the air. The fall seemed to last a lot longer than just a couple of seconds, but he hit the top of the outhouse at the exact spot he'd planned and sucked his knees to his chest and rolled just like the airborne instructors had taught him at Bragg. His aim was spectacular.

It was everything after it that went wrong.

Trapp felt the solid structure of the outhouse disappearing from underneath him as his momentum pulled him over the edge. He had just enough time to mutter, "Crap" before he skidded off, falling the last five feet to the ground and landing heavily on his back. He stared up at the sky, sucking air into winded lungs, and watched as Sikorski jumped considerably more nimbly, then slithered to the ground beside him.

"That's rough." Sikorski winced.

Sucking a breath, Trapp accepted his friend's proffered forearm and hauled himself back upright.

The wall around the home's backyard was only about shoulder high, at least for Trapp. Sikorski had to raise himself on his tiptoes as the two men surveyed the scene in front of them. In front was a narrow lane, on the other side of which was another row of houses that backed onto the river. A narrow, trash-filled alley ran between two of them, presumably leading right to the water.

"Give me a lift," Sikorski whispered.

Trapp dropped to one knee and boosted his friend to the top, then once more called on his forearm in order to climb up himself. They dropped quietly onto the road and brought their weapons back up. Trapp swept the street to the left as Sikorski did the same on the right. The street was littered with garbage: mostly sheet plastic and discarded drinks containers. Moving without dislodging any of it—and thus betraying their position —was painstaking and exhausting work.

The two operators communicated through body language alone as they crept across the street, hunched low over their weapons. Long months of training, working, and fighting together proved their worth as the two men worked like a single organism. They converged on either side of the alleyway that led to the river. Trapp wished he had a way of knowing if and where the insurgents had prepared fighting positions to cover their escape.

But now was not a time for wishing.

He tapped his chest, then flashed a two-finger gesture down the alley and waited for Sikorski to signal his agreement. No enemy general could have designed a better spot for an ambush. The passage was no more than a foot and a half wide —and narrower at points, so tight that Trapp would have to advance with his left shoulder arrowed in front of his right just to squeeze through. If a single gunman was waiting at the other end or even heard the sound of movement and got curious, they would be able to snuff out the threat to their rear in an instant.

On the other hand, it wasn't like there was another choice.

Trapp took a step forward. The walls of the buildings on either side of the alley weren't built straight, but rather angled slightly outward the higher they rose, making it feel more like a tunnel than a path. The thick walls seemed to muffle the sound of the vicious fight still raging in the village behind them.

He flashed the IR beam on the end of his rifle downward to reveal the trash blocking his route. He picked his way through step by step, the adrenaline pumping through his veins urging him to go faster and years of training pulling on the reins to make sure he didn't.

Halfway. Still no sign of the enemy. But maybe the sound of hushed voices on the other end.

He tried to glance back but couldn't. Not without turning his entire frame and cracking the AK over his shoulder against an adjacent wall loud enough to wake the dead. The only way out was forward.

Another foot forward, then another. He was two feet away from the end. The voices were louder now, more distinct, though he didn't understand a damn word of what was being said. A splash of water and a grunt of effort.

"Dammit," a familiar voice sounded on the radio, panting as though he'd just run a marathon. It was Muniz. "The boats are no good. Someone slashed them."

It was all the proof that Trapp needed. The insurgents had Breyer, and they also had a way of getting him out of the village. They would only need to move him a few miles downriver, just far enough to punch through the US military cordon around the settlement. Without any way of chasing them or aerial surveillance to follow them from above, Breyer might never be seen again.

He reached the end.

A narrow patch of gloom suddenly swallowed him whole. He stopped a few inches inside the alleyway and slowed his breathing to listen.

Another splash. They were launching a boat. Maybe two. He crept forward until his goggles jutted out of the alleyway.

There were over half a dozen men out there, maneuvering a pair of Zodiac-style rib boats into the water. Each had a powerful-looking outboard motor at the back. Three of the men crouched facing outward in Trapp's direction and held their weapons ready to fire.

And on the ground at their feet was the dark outline of a man. He was as still as the dead, though Trapp hoped fervently that wasn't the case. Since his wrists and ankles were bound, it seemed unlikely. But with a friendly in the firing line, Trapp couldn't risk starting a gunfight for fear of the consequences.

Shit.

This tactical situation was going from bad to worse.

"We've located Breyer," Sikorski's hushed voice transmitted over the net a moment later. "They're taking him out by boat. We need assistance immediately, over."

"This is Echo," another voice replied. "We're pinned down here and taking heavy casualties. We cannot move from our location at this time."

"Fuck," swore the commander of the Fox detachment. "I can send half my guys your way. But that's all. We've been engaged en route to Echo's position. It'll take a couple of minutes."

"I don't think we have that long," Sikorski replied.

Trapp turned around and gestured for his fellow Ranger to join him. They conferred in low, barely audible tones.

"I guess it's up to us," he whispered. "They just loaded him into the first of two boats, and four of them look like they're climbing in. All armed. That leaves three hanging around the second boat. Maybe a delaying force. But this is the only shot I think we're gonna get."

"You want us to chase them on our own?"

"Don't see how we have any other choice."

Sikorski shrugged. "Sure, why the hell not."

16

Trapp reached up and as silently as possible unclasped his helmet strap before lifting the Kevlar bowl off his head and placing it onto the alley floor. He detached the night vision goggles before standing back up. Sikorski looked at him as though he was crazy before a flash of understanding blossomed in his eyes.

In the darkness, the silhouette of a helmet was a dead giveaway that they were soldiers, not fellow insurgents. If they were going to stand any chance at getting onto that second boat without alerting those in the first that they had been compromised, then they needed to get close enough to dispatch them silently.

He waited until Sikorski did the same, then unclipped the rifle from his chest and set it on the ground next to the helmets, unlooping the strap of the AK from his shoulder in its place. The rifle felt unfamiliar in his grasp, but he'd fired them before. A cursory examination in the darkness indicated that it was in good working order. You had to put a rifle like this through hell before it wouldn't fire. He unclipped the flap over the hilt of his knife but didn't remove it from its sheath.

A throaty cough, then a low roar echoed over the surface of the river as the first of the boats started up. They didn't have much time. Water frothed underneath the outboard's blades, and it started to pick up speed. He lifted the scope to his eye and saw that the three men with the second boat were pushing it out onto the water.

None of them looked back.

A single, curt nod indicated to Sikorski that it was time to go. They didn't exchange a single word. There was no need. Either this plan succeeded, or very shortly, they would both be dead.

The two men exited the alleyway, Trapp feeling surprisingly naked without the protection of his helmet. A light breeze tugged at his sweat-soaked hair before dying completely, teasing without completion.

The first boat was already twenty yards away. Then another ten as its lead built with every passing second. They needed to move faster, or all this would be for nothing.

Muffled grunts echoed from up ahead as the insurgents manhandled the second boat into the water. They were only a few feet away now. He gritted his teeth as he prepared his battered, exhausted body for a fresh bout of combat.

Taking a deep breath, he sprinted for the men at the second boat. One turned his head, and Trapp imagined a narrowing of his eyes as he tried to make out what was coming toward him in the dark.

It was too late.

Trapp's boots splashed into the lapping water at the river's edge. The first foot sank about half a foot deep. He drew the stock of the AK back and smashed it into the unlucky insurgent's face, feeling the crunch of bone reverberating through the weapon's wood and metal frame. The man fell into the river without another sound, his head slipping below the waterline.

To Trapp's right, Sikorski did the same, swinging his rifle

like a club and knocking his target into the boat. The third man, standing in water as deep as his waist, reached inside the boat for a weapon. Trapp took a step forward to cut him off but immediately sank into the thick mud at the bottom of the river.

He ditched the Kalashnikov, reaching instead for his knife. He pulled it free of its sheath at the exact moment that the insurgent's hands fell on his rifle. The man started to spin, equally affected by the weight of the water and mud.

Trapp slashed the knife to the extent of his reach, cutting across the man's body and gouging a deep wound into his right thigh. The insurgent let out a cry of pain, which provoked only irritation in Trapp. Didn't this idiot know that he needed silence?

He wrenched his left boot out of the mud and waded forward another pace, dragging the leg after him. The insurgent fell backward, scrabbling against the boat for support as his wounded leg gave way underneath him. He called out numbly for help, terrified eyes staring at Trapp as he pawed with his rifle as though his fingers had gone numb.

He started to bring the weapon up, but it was too late. The point of Trapp's knife entered his throat and drove directly through the larynx, punching through the spinal column before exiting the skin on the other side. He collapsed instantly, dragging Trapp's arm below the waterline before he was able to free the blade.

"Start the engine," Trapp called to Sikorski, figuring that they could speak now that the boat with Breyer in was already lost to the naked eye.

"Way ahead of you," came the reply as Sikorski climbed into the boat. A moment later, the engine coughed into life, and he revved it once, playing with the controls. "Good to go."

Trapp continued splashing through the river, the water climbing up the fabric of his uniform to well above the waterline. He grabbed the body of the insurgent he'd killed, now floating on the river surface, and dragged the man toward him.

"What the hell you doing, Jason?" Sikorski asked, revving the outboard a second time. "We need to move!"

Without answering, Trapp tore the keffiyeh headscarf off the man's head. It was soaking wet. He slung it over his shoulder, then turned to another of the floating bodies, where he repeated his task. Only then did he climb into the boat.

He looked at Sikorski expectantly. "What are you waiting for?"

"You're one weird dude, did I ever tell you that?"

Trapp chuckled, the sound quickly torn away from his lips by the wind already ripping past as his friend immediately gunned the outboard motor, asking it for every last morsel of power it could give. A contrail of foaming water was dug out of the dark river behind.

Leaning back, he wrung the liquid from the two headscarves, then reached over and handed one to Sikorski. "Put this on."

"What's the play here, Jason?" the Ranger asked once he was done looping the cloth over his head and shoulders. "The way I see it, a frontal approach won't work. There's four of them and two of us, and the bad guys have an ace in the hole."

Trapp bit his lip and shot Sikorski a grimace. "I'm prepared to admit I might not have fully thought this through."

"Great." Sikorski laughed freely, tipping his head back and letting the wind whip at the looted headscarf. "At least it's always interesting."

"Command, this is Hangman," Trapp said, punching his radio transmit button. "We are in pursuit of Breyer and his kidnappers. We have visual confirmation that he is in their hands. They are on the Alwand heading northeast at high speed. Four tangos. Over."

"Understood, Hangman," came an immediate reply. "We're

vectoring additional surveillance assets, but they are at least eight mikes out."

"Copy. Will advise changes. Hangman out."

Trapp swore loudly into the night, thankful for the roar the outboard engine was kicking out. He turned to Sikorski, gesturing at the antenna on his back. "If it takes that long, we'll be out of radio range."

"Agreed," Sikorski said grimly. "We're on our own."

The younger man guided the hijacked rib boat expertly through the double bend the River Alwand took just northeast of Ali Daud, slowing only enough to avoid spilling its precious cargo out onto the water before pushing down on the throttle once more. The waterway opened up, and as Trapp lifted the detached night vision scope to his eyes, he could just make out the insurgent boat in the distance.

"They've got half a mile on us," he said. "We're gaining, but not quickly."

He dropped the scope and reached into his chest pocket for a map of the area, extracting a small pen-sized flashlight with a red beam and making sure that it was out of sight before he clicked it on. He scanned the map.

"Looks like there are at least three or four roads that lead to the water's edge in the next five miles. It would have to be one of them. Carrying a hostage would take too much time. All of them are outside our cordon, and they all lead to the highway. Hell, Breyer could be in Iran within a couple hours."

That thought hadn't yet occurred to Trapp, and he saw the same was true of Sikorski. The younger man's fingers visibly tightened on the rudder.

"Doesn't really narrow it down much, though, does it?"

"No," he conceded. "But to offload him, they'll need to slow down. They'll do it before the offload point so they don't miss it. That gives us the time we need to catch up. You gotta figure there will be vehicles waiting there."

"And then what? We're still outnumbered—probably by more than we are now, if those cars have drivers. And the insurgents—"

"—Still have Breyer." Trapp nodded. "It'll be dicey, but it's our only shot. They'll have at least two vehicles. So we need to make sure we're in one of them."

JUST AS TRAPP thought that the sounds of the battle in Ali Daud were fading, the first of several thunderous airstrikes split the night sky asunder. Despite his intense focus on the speedboat still a hundred yards further up the narrow river, he couldn't help but turn as a bright flash lit up the sky.

"Get some," Sikorski muttered. The words came out with little of his usual panache. Even as the glow of the first airstrike faded, a second hit, once again for the briefest of moments illuminating the small, battle-scarred settlement in the middle of ass nowhere.

Trapp turned away, crouching low and once again focusing his night vision scope on the speedboat they were chasing. The river was almost still, but at this speed, it was impossible to keep his aim locked in. The little circle of clarity danced with every tiny vibration from the engine, and every few seconds bucked up and landed on the side of the riverbank or a tree half a click in the distance.

"Fuck," he whispered, struggling to get a glimpse of the boat racing ahead of them for even a second. The scope drifted over the watercraft for just an instant, but it was long enough to confirm that it contained four gunmen and one bound unmoving prisoner.

As he watched, it seemed as though the man with his hand on the boat's rudder began squinting in his direction. With his free hand, he seemed to be waving something in the air. Trapp's filthy, camo-painted face wrinkled up as he tried to work out what the hell the militant was attempting to communicate.

No sooner had the thought crossed his mind than the rib hit a submerged object—perhaps a floating piece of driftwood or trash. Not large enough to do any serious damage, but enough to ruin his view once again.

"Hangman, what's your status?" a voice said through his radio headset. It sounded weaker and fainter than it had just a few moments earlier. They were quickly approaching the limits of their radio range. In just a couple of minutes, they would be on their own.

"I have the hostage in sight," he radioed, stretching the truth slightly as he slipped his night vision set through a rubber loop on the front of his plate carrier. "What's the ETA on that Predator?"

The drone could act as a radio relay, he knew, sucking up their transmissions before broadcasting them on to military units further afield. If this harebrained rescue effort was to have any chance of success, they needed to be able to communicate with the cavalry. It wasn't exactly *impossible* that he and Sikorski might pull off an audacious attempt on their own, but their chances of success rounded down to zero.

Breyer might be an asshole, but Trapp didn't think he should die because of it.

"Still five minutes out. We're concerned it might just get shot down."

Trapp slapped the side of the rib with an open palm in frustration. "Who gives a shit? It's a hunk of fucking metal. Get it overhead, and do it fast. Is it armed?"

"It's carrying two Hellfire missiles," the radio operator confirmed after a brief delay.

"Best news I've heard all week," Sikorski said as he adjusted the boat's rudder just in time to swing them around a sharp bend in the river.

"Hangman, what's your location?"

Trapp resisted the urge to ask how the hell he should know. Instead, he reached into his pants pocket and pulled out his map of the area. He looked around for something to use to block any light emissions and found a ragged tarpaulin at the bottom of the boat. He ducked under it and pulled out a red flashlight.

"Sikorski, how fast you think we're going?"

His friend paused a beat before saying, "I guess fifteen or twenty knots. I make it about seven minutes so far."

"Christ," Trapp said under his breath a few seconds later as he dragged his finger along the map from Ali Daud, following the course of the River Alwand. They had already traveled several kilometers. That wouldn't be so bad, except for one particular line on the map about ten kilometers farther on.

The border with Iran.

He quickly radioed his best guess as to their present location to the operation's command post. There was a brief moment of silence as everybody seemed to realize at once that the kidnappers' most likely destination was foreign soil.

And if Breyer crossed the border into Iran, then there was likely very little that the US military could do to rescue him. The once-vaunted US Army was stretched almost a breaking point by its attempt to put out the thousands of violent sectarian brushfires that were consuming the dry kindling of post-Saddam Iraq. The likelihood of an American president greenlighting a rescue mission that might spark a far larger regional war was unlikely, to say the least.

"Hangman," the radio operator finally said, "your instructions are to maintain visual contact with the hostage takers. Do not engage. I repeat, do not engage. Once we get that Predator overhead, you will break off and return to Red Buffalo for evac. Do you copy?"

Trapp and Sikorski shared a disbelieving glance.

"What's the status of the QRF?"

"Ambushed on the way in."

"What other forces do we have en route?"

"We're working on it," the operator replied.

Trapp took his finger off the transmit button. "That means sweet fuck all, and you know it," he hissed. "The brass are worried about a Chinook getting shot down while loaded up with twenty operators. By the time they close out their pity party, it'll be too late. The insurgents will have Breyer over the border, and it's all over."

"So what do you want to do about it, Jason?" Sikorski asked, once again spinning the rib around a tight bend in the ancient river.

Looking back at his friend, Trapp tried to gauge exactly what it was that he was asking. To his surprise, he didn't just see the resolve that he'd expected on Sikorski's face, but something else. Belief.

More startling than that, it was directed at him.

"How do you feel about leaving a man behind?" he asked.

Sikorski shook his head. "Not real good, Jason. Not real good."

"Yeah, me neither," Trapp replied, twisting his neck as a change in the sound of the boat engine up ahead caught his attention. "How about we do something to change the equation?"

"Hangman, confirm your instructions," the radio operator said.

"I'm with you, buddy," Sikorski said. "Just say the word."

Trapp reached for his night vision scope. He flicked it on and brought it up to his eye. With Sikorski slowing their boat in line with the chase craft, it was easier to lock in on the kidnappers. Their speedboat was definitely slowing, though its engine still glowed a bright white through the thermal filter.

He raked the viewfinder up and down either bank of the

Alwand. There had to be a reason that the kidnappers were slowing. They had to be close to the vehicle transfer location. The thermal sight made finding it easy. Three large blobs of heat—much cooler than the engine of the speedboat but still easily visible—radiated out into the night.

"Command, I have three 4x4s in sight," he radioed without acknowledging their prior orders. "Looks like the bad guys are taking this over land."

A muffled scratching sound through his headset might or might not have been an answer. If it was, Trapp couldn't understand it. He shot Sikorski a worried look. "Looks like we're on our own."

17

The boat they were chasing visibly began to slow and turn toward the bank of the river. Instantly, Sikorski flared off their own speed. The last thing they needed was to make land too quickly. The roar of two sets of engines immediately faded. They were far enough now from Red Buffalo that the sounds of battle—even the airstrikes—were muted.

"You think they'll buy it?" Sikorski asked quietly, his lips barely moving as they floated downriver, moving little faster than the speed of the current.

"They won't wait for us," Trapp said confidently, hoping his read on the situation was correct. "If this Jafari guy is as professional as we think he is, Breyer's kidnappers will have instructions to get him across the border yesterday."

"I hope you're right..."

The enemy speedboat touched the riverbank a few yards downstream of the awaiting 4x4s. Trapp surreptitiously snapped his thermal scope back to his eye and watched as half a dozen men rushed to secure the boat and hustle its occupants onto dry land.

"Nine bad guys," he whispered, "including the guys on the boat."

"Not bad odds," Sikorski replied optimistically. He didn't even sound convinced himself.

One of the waiting militants dragged Breyer onto dry land, landing a sharp punch into the captive operator's ribs as he did so. A cry of pain echoed across the still water before it was quickly swallowed by the rumble of vehicle engines roaring into life.

"Assholes," Trapp muttered.

As he watched, Breyer was hustled into the lead vehicle, and half a dozen of the militants began climbing into the first two 4x4s in the short column. Trapp reported this over the radio, hoping that somebody out there was listening. When no response came, his mind was made up. They were definitely going to have to do this themselves.

"You want me to play dead?" he asked.

"No chance. You think I can carry your fat ass?" Sikorski retorted. "Besides, your Arabic's better than mine. Not that that's saying much."

Trapp stifled a chuckle. He crouched lower as he watched the first two vehicles begin to move, leaving just two of the militants and one vehicle left at the dirt track on the riverbank. One of the remaining two men was pacing up and down at the river's edge as the others stared out toward the two Americans. That one raised his arms above his head and began waving them in, calling something in a low voice that didn't make it to Trapp's ears.

He turned and gestured at the outboard engine on the back of the boat, as if indicating that it had suffered a mechanical fault. They needed to stretch this out for long enough to make sure that the first two vehicles got far enough away to ensure they didn't see the dirty work that was about to commence—

but not so far as to prevent him and Sikorski from catching back up.

It was a delicate dance.

Seeing that the first two SUVs were already fifteen or twenty yards away and picking up speed quickly, Trapp muttered to Sikorski to give the outboard a little gas. "Not too much. Don't want them to get suspicious."

Their boat drifted a little more quickly toward the riverbank. Ten yards, then five, then the nose bumped up against soft, silty earth. The two militants who had been left waiting for them scrambled to secure the boat and called for them to hurry. Both were armed – one with a rifle, the other only a pistol.

"Help," Trapp called out in Arabic, deliberately muffling his voice and pointing at Sikorski, who slumped at the back of the boat. He gestured at his own side, then pointed at Sikorski once again as if to indicate that he was injured. As he did so, he surreptitiously reached to his waist and drew his already-bloodied knife from its sheath.

He searched his Arabic vocabulary for a way of communicating with the two militants but thought better of it. Sikorski was right; he wasn't even in the same ZIP code as fluent.

One of the two men jumped onto the boat and clambered toward Sikorski. Trapp held his breath, hoping that the guy's rifle-toting buddy would do the same. A few rounds from that particular weapon would ruin everybody's day.

Unfortunately, they were shit out of luck. The guy on the riverbank was jumpy. He had his rifle up in a firing position and his neck on a stalk. He kept whipping his head around, searching for imaginary sounds.

The guy with the pistol was now only a couple of steps away from Sikorski, who lay back against the rubber sides of the rib clutching his stomach and groaning loudly. As the gunman closed in, he began speaking in concerned, rapid-fire, Arabic, clearly worried that Sikorski was seriously injured.

Don't oversell it, Trapp thought, bringing his right foot up onto the rib's rubber wall and tensing his thigh.

But what happened on the boat was no longer his fight. He kept his eyes on the shooter on the riverbank. Kept watching as the man reacted to some imaginary sound, spun around, and swept his rifle across the bone-dry fields behind him.

It was the only opening he was going to get. He thrust his right leg down hard, driving all his power through his planted foot and slingshotted himself up toward the bank. The militant reacted, but not quickly enough as Trapp drew his right hand back, his fingers wrapped tightly around the handle of his knife.

As his target's head swung around and a pair of startled eyes locked on to Trapp's own, the Ranger bounded toward him in one long, rapid stride before sinking the blade to the hilt into his stomach. Before the man had a chance to react, before he could so much as let out a yelp of pain, Trapp pulled the blade free of his flesh and drove it through his Adam's apple.

The first wound would have been fatal eventually.

But the second dropped him instantly.

The rifle fell from his suddenly nerveless grip, and he clutched ineffectually at his throat for a couple of seconds before the blood loss proved too great.

Trapp kicked the weapon out of reach and then spun back toward Sikorski. He needn't have bothered. The other militant had crouched down to check his friend's supposed wounds and had paid for his charity with his life. Sikorski rolled out from underneath the man's body and withdrew his knife from the underside of the guy's chin. The front of his fatigues, already soaked by filthy river water up to the upper thigh, were now black with blood.

"Let's get moving," Trapp said hurriedly, wiping the blade of his knife on his pants before returning it to its sheath.

He turned back to the body of the man he'd just killed and ran his hands up and down the corpse's clothing searching for anything useful. He came up empty but grabbed the man's rifle and a spare magazine, which he stuffed into his combat webbing with the others.

"Right behind you."

The two men rushed for the empty SUV. It was an old Toyota Land Cruiser. The engine wasn't running, but the keys were in the ignition. Trapp twisted them, depressed the clutch, and pushed the ancient gearbox through its paces as quickly as he dared. Thankfully, it sounded like it was in pretty good condition.

"NASA shouldn't bother sending those rovers to Mars," Sikorski said as he reached for his thermal scope. "Just send one of these babies and save the taxpayer a few million bucks."

Trapp gunned the Land Cruiser down the dirt track as fast as he dared. There was barely any light in the sky, barring the reflected glow from a nearby city about five miles down the road. Neither of the two 4x4s they were chasing had used their headlights, so neither did he. Turning them on would have been a dead giveaway.

"How far behind are we?" he asked.

"Maybe a hundred yards," Sikorski said. "Hard to be sure."

"We can't lose them," Trapp replied unnecessarily, feeling the pressure of the task ahead of them weighing down on his shoulders.

The next couple of minutes—before the replacement Predator drone came on station in the skies overhead—would be critical. If he and Sikorski lost touch and the militants managed to get close enough to the nearby city to blend in with other road traffic, then the game was over. He couldn't remember what the place was called but knew that it had tens of thousands of inhabitants. Finding Breyer in that warren would be a hopeless task.

"Sharp left in ten yards," Sikorski said urgently.

Trapp reacted on instinct like a rally driver reacting to his navigator's instructions, stamping on the brakes and spinning the wheel in the direction indicated. Even with his pupils fully dilated and his entire attention on the bumpy dirt track up ahead, it was almost impossible to make out more than a couple of feet ahead of him without night vision. And since both men had discarded their helmets, he had no way of mounting his own scope to his face.

He was just going to have to trust his friend.

"Straight, about fifty yards," Sikorski said.

The two men settled into an easy rhythm. They had operated together long enough for each to trust the other implicitly, which was the only way that this could work. After about half a kilometer, the rutted farm track met the more level surface of a dirt road. Up ahead, Trapp just barely made out two sets of brake lights in the distance before they disappeared around a turning.

"Look at the map," he said, moving up into fourth gear and stepping on the gas. "I've got this. Try and find out where the hell they might be going."

Sikorski dropped his scope onto his lap and did as instructed, pulling out a red flashlight and clicking it on before cursing when the beam failed to ignite. Trapp reached up and flicked on the cabin's interior light, gritting his teeth as the glow cost him his natural night vision.

"Okay, okay..." Sikorski muttered, his full attention on the oiled map on his lap. He traced his finger from the river across a nest of thin lines. "Looks like this road takes us to that city near the border. It's called, uh, Tolafarush."

"How far from there to Iran?"

"About ten clicks."

Trapp hissed with frustration as he pushed the Land Cruiser about as far as he dared in the dark. A couple of minutes passed in silence as they spun around corners, occasionally glimpsing sets of brake lights in the almost pitch blackness of the Iraqi night. It seemed as though they were gaining on Breyer's kidnappers.

But not by much.

Sikorski attempted to radio their location and estimate of the kidnappers' destination to the command post but received no response. When that failed, he once again glued the night vision scope to his eye and began bellowing rally instructions. Trapp slipped into fifth gear. Going at that speed on a road this terrible without headlights was an insane decision.

But it was also the right one.

They started gaining more quickly. By the time they reached a small settlement of a couple hundred mostly dark houses, they were only twenty or thirty yards behind the first two vehicles in their convoy. Trapp eased off the gas, careful never to get close enough to the rear vehicle to allow anyone inside to get a glimpse at him and Sikorski.

"How far to Tolafarush?" Trapp asked, shifting back down into third and letting an ancient pickup truck slip between the first two SUVs and his vehicle. There was more traffic on the road here, and he used it to his advantage.

Before the Ranger could answer, both men's headsets crackled with an incoming transmission. "Hangman, Chopper, do you copy?"

"It's good to hear your voice," Sikorski replied.

"We have another MQ-1 in the air. It's close enough to relay your radios. What is your current location?"

Sikorski read off his best estimate of their current map grid square. There was a short delay before the radio operator said, "You were instructed to return to Red Buffalo."

"Negative," Sikorski replied quickly. "We did not receive

that instruction. We are in pursuit of Breyer's kidnappers. We are in the third of a convoy of three Toyota Land Cruiser SUVs."

"Repeat your last, Chopper," the operator said, sounding distinctly strained.

Sikorski did so. This time, the pause was longer. "You will break off and return to Red Buffalo."

"Negative," Sikorski practically shouted through his headset before Trapp had a chance to do the same. "If we lose Breyer now, we'll never get him back."

"The Predator will be overhead in about three minutes," the operator said. "We can take it from here."

"Tell them not to get too close," Trapp warned. "If they get wise they're being watched, this might get hairy. Besides, we need eyes on the ground. If they get him into a tunnel or switch vehicles, we'll lose him."

"Listen to me," Sikorski snarled. "You back that drone the hell off, understood? I will keep you in the loop with minute-by-minute updates on our location. When we return to Anaconda, we'll accept whatever disciplinary sanction the colonel sees fit. Until then, you will back our play or I'm turning off this radio. Understood?"

18

C ompared to the backwater of Ali Daud, the streets of Tolafarush seemed almost overwhelmingly busy, even at this late hour. Large trucks packed with farm produce rumbled up and down, and mopeds and motorcycles accelerated through the traffic with euphoric disregard for the safety of their riders.

Trapp maintained a steady gap from the back of the second Land Cruiser but never took his eyes off it. According to the radio operator, it would be almost an hour until fresh units could be choppered to this hotspot. The only friendly military force nearby was a Kurdish militia, and Trapp wasn't sure he wanted to trust Breyer's rescue to the local neighborhood watch.

It was therefore critical that he and Sikorski worked out which vehicle Breyer was riding in. If the kidnappers were heading right for the border, then they might only get a short window in which to try and snatch the captured Delta commando back. Every detail might be key to evening the odds.

Especially since it was only a twenty-minute drive to the border, meaning the two Rangers in their battered Land

Cruiser might end up being the only rescue party Breyer was going to get.

"You think they'll go to ground?" Sikorski muttered, squinting at the back window of the SUV up ahead.

"What would you do in their shoes?"

"They must know that we'll flood the entire area with troops until we get him back. The brass will have us kicking down every door in a fifty-mile radius if that's what it takes."

"Then you have your answer," Trapp said grimly.

Sikorski swallowed hard. The conclusion was clear: The cavalry weren't going to arrive in time. "So it's up to us?"

"Looks like it."

"Shit."

Trapp peered at the SUV they were following. "You see that?"

Sikorski muttered his agreement. There was movement by the rear window. It looked like somebody was twisting in their seat and gesturing in their direction. "Looks like they're trying to communicate with us."

"You think they've figured out we aren't who they think we are?"

"If they don't know already, they will soon."

"Agreed," Trapp muttered, reflexively squeezing and releasing his grip on the steering wheel. He dropped back a few more yards, but even as he did so, the SUV's rear window opened, and a hand was thrust out. "What's he holding?"

"Looks like a radio," Sikorski replied. "You were right."

Trapp swore under his breath. "You find a handset on either of those tangos we took down?"

Sikorski shook his head. As he did so, he reached forward and opened the glove box. Inside there was a Motorola radio handset. He removed it and started fiddling with the volume knob. As he did so, the hand in the SUV they were following drew back inside. A moment later, a burst of rapidfire, strained Arabic erupted inside the Land Cruiser's cabin.

"Care to translate?" Sikorski asked, thrusting it in Trapp's direction.

"I top out at hello," he replied, making a face as he tried to work out what to do next. He backed off the gas as a thought occurred to him.

"What are you doing?" Sikorski said. "We'll lose them!"

Trapp scanned the road up ahead. They had already passed through the bulk of the urban area the convoy had entered. "We must be on the other side of Tolafarush by now, right?"

"Yeah..."

"Then it's a straight road right up to the border. If they didn't ditch their vehicles by now, I doubt they're going to."

"So what?"

"So we lose 'em," Trapp said. As the rearmost of the two Land Cruisers ahead of them disappeared around a sharp turn in the road up ahead, he stamped on the brakes and brought their vehicle to a dead stop. "Come on. We're moving."

With a shocked expression on what little of his face Trapp could see behind the keffiyeh wrapped around it, Sikorski followed. He grabbed the radio handset and his rifle and jumped out of the car. "What the hell are we doing?"

Trapp explained on the move, scanning the oncoming traffic as he brought up his rifle. "We need two cars. Something inconspicuous so we can get close enough to figure out which vehicle Breyer is in."

Half a dozen oncoming cars screeched to a halt, brakes smoking. The closest to Trapp began to reverse, but he sprinted toward it with his rifle's muzzle aimed at the driver. After a moment's hesitation, Sikorski aped his movements, picking out a vehicle of his own.

Trapp wrenched the driver's side door of his chosen ride open and heaved the hapless man behind the wheel out onto the street. In an ideal world, there was a form that the guy could've filled out to pay for restitution of his property. But there wasn't time for that.

He forced himself into the tiny sedan car. It had almost half a million miles on the clock but was somehow still going—an everyday miracle of Japanese engineering. A quick glance at the rearview mirror showed that Sikorski was already inside a battered pickup truck, whose driver was nowhere to be seen.

"Time to get out of here," he radioed. "The Kurds are pretty big on the right to bear arms, and grand theft auto is definitely a capital crime in this neck of the woods."

"Understood."

It took a couple of minutes to catch up with the now abbreviated convoy of Land Cruisers, which were now racing through what traffic there was on the streets, making liberal use of their horns.

"I think they figured it out," Sikorski commented.

Trapp backed off the gas when he was about fifty yards away from the rearmost SUV. He cursed as he realized that his hastily chosen vehicle sat low to the ground. It would be almost impossible to see inside.

He switched to the command radio net. "Command, we are about seven clicks out from the Iranian border. The bad guys are running for cover. We need to interdict them before they reach the crossing or we lose Breyer."

The radio operator no longer wasted time berating the two Rangers for their tactical decisions. "What's your recommendation, Hangman?"

"How long to get that Predator overhead?"

Trapp slipped into fourth gear and accelerated past the last of four cars that separated him with the last Land Cruiser as he waited for the response. Thankfully, pretty much everybody in Iraq drove like a maniac, so his driving wouldn't necessarily attract unwanted attention.

"Sixty seconds."

"Do it. And get authorization to target one of the two SUVs on my command, understood?"

"Which one? Do you have eyes on Breyer?"

"Negative. Working on it. Just get the damn authorization. We're only going to get one shot at this."

Another mile marker flashed by. Trapp eased past another of the cars.

"What's the play here, Trapp?" Sikorski asked, his tone ragged with stress.

"You need to get close. Figure out which vehicle Breyer's riding in. When we know, we're going to have to split the bad guys up. And then things might get a little bit spicy."

"You're a maniac, Sergeant," Sikorski radioed. But despite everything, he sounded a little impressed. "Moving into position."

Trapp reached for the Kalashnikov he'd left on the passenger seat and stowed it out of sight but in easy reach. He knew it was loaded, and the safety was already dealt with.

"MQ-1 is thirty seconds to visual range."

He overtook another vehicle. Now only two cars, plus Sikorski's pickup truck, were ahead of him and the kidnappers. His palms were slick on the steering wheel, and he reached down to his pants and wiped each of them in turn. It did little good.

By now, Sikorski was only ten or fifteen yards behind the rear Toyota. His vehicle rode high enough off the ground that he would be almost level with the cabins of the two SUVs. That meant he would be able to peer inside. But they were sure to return the favor.

Black smoke poured out of the pickup truck's exhaust pipe as Sikorski accelerated toward the kidnappers. He veered wildly into the left-hand lane to overtake the rear Toyota. His driving was so insane that it was sure to attract unwanted attention. He whipped right past it and headed to the front of the convoy.

"What the hell are you doing?" Trapp hissed to himself.

For about fifteen seconds, Sikorski's truck drove side by side with the first Toyota. Trapp cursed his ancient sedan, which was barely able to keep up the pursuit. He had no idea what was happening up ahead.

"I didn't see him up there," he reported.

Trapp kept his eyes glued to the rear Toyota. The driver made no change to his speed or course, which he hoped meant that Sikorski's attention hadn't been noticed.

"Predator is overhead. Tracking two SUVs approximately three clicks from the border crossing," the radio operator reported. Trapp was so drunk on adrenaline he barely heard the man's words.

Sikorski switched back into the left-hand lane and braked hard. The frontmost Land Cruiser whipped past once again. This time, the Ranger drove alongside the rearmost Toyota. Trapp held his breath as the seconds ticked by as he waited for his friend to report. The silence seemed to stretch out into eternity.

"I see him!"

"You sure?" Trapp radioed, reaching for his rifle. "Because if not..."

"No I'm not fucking sure," Sikorski shouted over the net. "I got one look. But we don't have a choice. Punch it."

Trapp stepped on the gas. Though he hadn't discussed a precise plan with Sikorski, there was only one way this could really go. They needed to separate the vehicle that was carrying Breyer from the other SUV. And that was going to take a little offensive driving.

"Command, target the leading Land Cruiser," he radioed. "Fire on my instruction only, understood?"

"Hangman, confirm no friendlies inside."

"Confirmed," Trapp replied, feeling a chill run down his spine.

A lot was riding on Sikorski's brief glance into the Toyota's cabin. But they didn't have a choice. The concrete structures of the border crossing were in sight now. To either side was a thin chain-link fence. He had no idea whether the land around the border was mined—it wouldn't be surprising given the torturous recent history Iraq had with its largest neighbor—but if not, it would be child's play to avoid the crossing point entirely.

As Trapp accelerated past the rear Land Cruiser, the bad guys finally seemed to figure out that something was up. He watched as the barrel of a rifle smashed through the rear windowpane, spraying glass all across the road before the hood of his car ate up the damage.

He saw the flash of gunfire and tensed himself for impact. They had him at a disadvantage: they could fire at him, but not the other way around.

Not with Breyer inside.

All three rounds in the burst went wide. But before Trapp could breathe a sigh of relief, the rifle's muzzle seemed to lengthen as a spout of white exhaust gases exploded out of it. This time one of the bullets smashed through his windshield, causing opaque spiderwebs to block out the view from the entire passenger side.

"Fuck," he muttered as he stepped on the gas, slipping up into fifth gear the second the engine was able to. He pushed the pedal all the way to the floor and wrenched the wheel suddenly to the side, guiding his sedan into the other lane.

And not a moment too soon.

Another burst of gunfire erupted from the back of the rear Land Cruiser, stitching the air his head had occupied an instant earlier. If Trapp had enough mental bandwidth to spare offering a prayer, he would have begged for Breyer to slip free of his restraints and punch the shooter's lights out.

But the big man wasn't on call. This was a matter of free will.

Somehow, the decrepit Japanese sedan started gaining on the far more powerful—yet more heavily loaded—SUV. He crept up to the side of the other vehicle and drove parallel alongside it.

"You ready, Sikorski?" he radioed, his chest tight from the exertion of pushing the car to its limits. Once again, his palms were slick on the steering wheel, and as he glanced to his side to check whether somebody was about to start shooting at him again, a droplet of salty sweat stung his eyesight.

"You bet your ass," his partner replied, sounding as relaxed as if he was out for a Sunday drive.

Trapp drew in a deep breath and squinted through his blurred vision. "Now!"

19

The instant Trapp gave the command, he spun his steering wheel to the side and sideswiped his sedan against the much heavier Land Cruiser. The tiny car bounced off as though it was a toy, windows shattering all along the affected side, but the unexpected action caused the Toyota's driver to act on instinct. He swerved toward the concrete lane divider in an attempt to get away from the lunatic hell-bent on crashing both of them.

At the very same time, Sikorski braked hard up ahead.

The Land Cruiser ran into the back of the other Ranger's pickup truck, but the weight disparity between the two vehicles was much less pronounced. Sikorski's vehicle was shunted forward only a few additional yards, but the action forced the driver of Breyer's getaway vehicle to slow in an attempt to avoid a more serious collision.

Trapp gritted his teeth and fed the sedan's steering wheel back toward the Land Cruiser that he and Sikorski now had boxed in. Once again, his friend stamped on the brakes, and without the advantage of speed and momentum, the Toyota had much less power to play with. This time, his sedan was able to push it to the side.

Almost immediately, a gap opened up between the kidnappers' two vehicles. Ten yards, then twenty, then thirty. The lead vehicle built up a lead of almost fifty yards before its driver belatedly recognized the problem and started to slow.

"Command," Trapp grunted the second he saw that the plan had worked. "Take out the lead SUV. Now!"

He held his breath even as his heart raced from the effort of holding his sedan against the struggling Land Cruiser. Its driver had finally figured out what the hell was going on and was once again attempting to accelerate. Up ahead, Sikorski looked to have his pickup truck in the lowest possible gear, and his foot stamped hard on the brake. Clouds of white smoke were pouring off his tires as the Toyota attempted to push him out the way. Brass round casings were raining down in every direction as the SUV's occupants fired wildly—and thankfully blindly.

"Come on," he muttered underneath his breath, praying for the Predator's weapon operator not to fumble the ball. Already the lead SUV had slowed almost to a complete stop. Another few seconds and he would be able to spin the vehicle around and race toward his stricken comrade.

At that point, the game was up. With their inability to return fire in case they caught Breyer in the crossfire, Trapp and Sikorski would be sitting ducks.

Almost seventy yards farther down the road, the SUV came to a dead stop. It seemed to rest there for a moment, though perhaps that was only Trapp's overactive imagination playing tricks. A rush of horror overcame him as, with his own sedan squealing from the cumulative weight of multiple sidelong impacts from the Land Cruiser as it struggled to wrench free, he watched the other SUV execute a rapid three-point turn and begin to accelerate back toward him.

He blinked. With the back of his left arm, he wiped the sweat that was stinging his eyes. He blinked again.

With a streak of smoke and flame, a Hellfire missile roared out of the night sky and destroyed the lead SUV. One moment it was there, the next it was gone. A couple of seconds after that, fragments of metal and plastic and glass started raining down out of the sky, plinking off of Trapp's already shattered windscreen and the roof of his vehicle.

Without even giving himself enough time to think, he reached for the rifle that was resting against the driver's side door. His stomach clenched with nerves, so tight he was barely able to breathe.

"Let's do this," he heard Sikorski radio through his headset as his friend jumped out of his pickup truck. The three vehicles were still moving, but now only at a couple of miles an hour as the trapped Land Cruiser struggled to push against the combined weights of two other vehicles.

But now that Sikorski was no longer behind the wheel of his truck, that wouldn't last.

Time seemed to slow. Trapp flung his car door open and felt the impact of his boots thudding against the concrete road surface. He was vaguely aware of an inferno farther down the road as flames swallowed what was left of the kidnappers' other vehicle. Thick, acrid smoke stung his nostrils and lungs as he inhaled a toxic soup of burning chemicals.

Another tick for the VA disability scorecard.

As Trapp spun, bringing his rifle up to his shoulder and sighting it on the now battered and dented Land Cruiser, he saw Sikorski out of the corner of his eye vault onto the bed of the pickup truck and fire three single rounds through the driver's side windshield.

"Jesus," Trapp muttered, hoping his friend was certain that Breyer wasn't in the firing line. Even a single unlucky ricochet...

But he knew Sikorski too well to doubt him. If he had fired

at the driver, that meant Breyer was very likely to be in the rear row of seats on the passenger side. He had to work on that basis, anyway.

As he closed within a few feet of the Land Cruiser, still shielded by his own near-totaled sedan, Trapp drank in the full picture of the scene. Both doors on the passenger side were smashed and crunched beyond repair and almost certainly could not be opened. He heard another report from Sikorski's weapon but had no sense from this angle of what he was firing at.

A rifle opened up on full automatic. Trapp ducked just as a bullet whipped past his left ear. Instantly, he placed the gunshots as coming from the shooter in the trunk/cargo compartment at the rear of the Land Cruiser—the guy who had shot at him during the pursuit.

The second the shooter's magazine ran dry, Trapp popped up and fired two bursts a couple of feet over the roof of the SUV to keep the gunman pinned. He switched the AK-47 into single-shot mode and sprinted toward the vehicle. Shards of shattered glass surrounded the punched-out rear window. Right behind was the silhouette of a man.

He was fumbling to reload his rifle.

Too slow, buddy.

Just as Trapp heard the telltale click that indicated a new magazine had been pushed home, he reversed his own weapon and rammed its stock through the space where the rear windshield used to be. It made a pleasing crack as it collided with the shooter's forehead, blacking him out instantly.

Maybe killing him as well. Trapp didn't have time to check.

Ignoring the now out-of-action kidnapper in the back of the SUV, Trapp rapidly sidestepped around the vehicle to the driver's side. Unlike the side he'd repeatedly smashed his car into, the chassis and doors on the opposite side were relatively undamaged.

"One shooter left," Sikorski called out, his voice hoarse as a result of the smoke tearing his lungs and the adrenaline pumping through his veins. "Back seats. Fucker's got a gun to Breyer's head."

"Got it," Trapp said tersely right as he came level with the rear window, his rifle aimed at the skull of the last remaining shooter. Out of the corner of his left eye, he saw the silhouettes of two men in the front seats. Since Sikorski still had the high ground from the bed of his pickup, he guessed they were both deceased.

Breyer appeared to be unconscious but hopefully not dead. He was bound by his wrists and ankles and a scrap of cloth wrapped around the back of his head indicated he was probably gagged, too. His large frame was almost implausibly stuffed into the foot well of the rear row of seats, his neck at a hinky angle.

"You speak English?" Trapp snapped as his eyes grew accustomed to the gloom inside the vehicle. The remaining shooter was covered in his dead comrade's blood and held a handgun between his knees aimed at the back of Breyer's head.

His hand was trembling. As Trapp spoke, the man drew in a sharp breath.

"I'll take that as a yes," Trapp continued.

He took one step to the left so that he could be sure that if he fired, the round would pass through the kidnapper's head and right out the back of the Toyota without ricocheting off anything that could potentially endanger the hostage.

A beam of moonlight illuminated the shooter's face as he did so. Instantly Trapp placed who he was talking to. It was Omar, Nadia's abusive husband—and the guy who had put a gun to his own son Abdel's head.

This wasn't the first time he had tangled with this asshole.

For an instant, Trapp resisted the urge to squeeze the Kalashnikov's trigger and splinter the bastard's forehead. In his peripheral vision, he could see that Omar's finger was on the trigger of his firearm but probably without sufficient pressure that an involuntary jerk after being shot would prematurely end Breyer's vacation on planet Earth.

Probably.

"What's the play here, Jason?" Sikorski whispered through their radio link.

Trapp ignored him, consciously forcing himself to expel his anger and tension at the sight of Omar. It wasn't just Breyer's life on the line here. There was an innocent child to think of.

"I'm going to open this door," Trapp said, gesturing at the rear passenger door.

"Don't! I'll shoot him," Omar threatened, waving his pistol.

"No you won't," Trapp said calmly, taking a step back and gently tugging open the handle. It was a judgment call. This was a high-stress situation. Anything could tip Omar over the edge.

Hopefully not this.

"Put down the gun, Omar," Trapp said, displaying his knowledge of the man's name for the first time.

A slight widening of Omar's eyes indicated it had hit home. "You kill me if I do."

"No I won't. You still have leverage."

As Omar's forehead wrinkled with confusion, his aim jerked upward a few inches.

"I got a shot, Jason," Sikorski radioed. Trapp surreptitiously gestured at his friend to stand down. He inhaled sharply, hoping he'd made the right decision.

"What leverage?" Omar snapped.

"Your son, Abdel. I'll let you walk out of here if you tell me where he is."

20

"You have got to be shitting me," Sikorski groaned from inside the cabin as the battered, barely functioning pickup truck rolled to a halt in front of the old police station that had been taken over by the local Kurdish militia for use as their headquarters.

Trapp hid his own disappointment at the welcoming party. It consisted of half a dozen men in their fifties and sixties, one of whom was using a Mosin-Nagant bolt-action rifle as a walking stick.

Barrel down.

"That gun's gotta be a hundred years old," Sikorski said, gesturing at the antique weapon as though there was any way he could have missed noticing it.

"Eyes on the prize, bud," Trapp called out loudly from the bed of the truck, where he was covering Omar at the same time as attempting to administer basic first aid to Breyer, who was stretched out—still unconscious.

"Yes, boss," his partner said as he climbed out of the truck.

Now that the wind noise from the whistle stop journey back from the Iranian border into the center of Tolafarush had quieted, Trapp gestured at Breyer and flashed Omar a mean look. "Did you drug him?"

The Iraqi was still holding a pistol, though Trapp guessed he was even less likely to use it than he had been before. He was outnumbered eight to one now, and that didn't count any more Kurdish militiamen who were still inside the police station.

"Yes," Omar confirmed, his throat as raw from the grit and pollution in the air as Trapp's was. "He won't wake up for hours."

"You better hope he does," Sikorski snapped as the welcoming party approached.

"That wasn't the deal," the Iraqi protested.

"Well, it fucking is now," Sikorski continued, menacingly gesturing with his pistol.

"Can it," Trapp said. "Help me get Breyer out. I don't like him out in the open like this. Anybody could take a potshot."

He grabbed Omar by the shoulder. "You take his legs."

The Iraqi bared his teeth, but another intense glare from Trapp silenced whatever he was about to say. The Kurds didn't speak English—at least not this party of grandfathers—but they seemed to know who Trapp and Sikorski were and what was asked of them. A couple of minutes of strenuous effort later, Breyer was inside the police station. Trapp noted to his relief that there were a couple of dozen younger Kurds inside, many of whom were armed with automatic weapons.

"Geez," Sikorski muttered, running his knuckles down the inside of the station's thick concrete walls. "You could drop a nuke on this place and I reckon it would barely make a dent."

"Let's hope it doesn't come to that," Trapp muttered. He saw what looked very much like a weapons locker and strode toward it, dumping the half-empty magazine from his Kalashnikov and replacing it in his webbing with several more, courtesy of the Kurds.

"You think the Iranians might try and snatch him back?" Sikorski asked. He cast an uneasy glance in Omar's direction, though the Iraqi was well covered by several mean-looking Kurds.

Trapp ignored him momentarily. "Command, what's the status on our extraction? Brian needs medical assistance. We believe he's been sedated. As far as I can tell, he has no physical injuries, beyond a nasty gash on his forehead and a few cuts and scrapes."

"Copy your last, Hangman," the operator answered a few moments later. "1st Battalion, 9th Cav is en route from FOB Normandy, company strength. They're thirty mikes out and hauling ass."

Spinning back to Sikorski, Trapp stabbed his index finger against the man's vest. He then gestured at Breyer and said, "You don't take your fucking eyes off of him, you understand?"

"Hey," his friend replied, looking slightly affronted behind his mask of stubble, dirt, sweat and exhaustion. "This is a team effort. We got this far, didn't we?"

"I'm going after the kid," Trapp said.

His body ached. His fatigues were still damp from wading through the river, his boots squelched with every step, and somehow silt and filth had made it into his socks. Every inch of his skin stung from some nick, cut, scrape, or contusion. His neck hurt, and he barely had enough energy to lift his rifle. The sane part of his brain was screaming at him to stay here, inside the station's thick walls and wait for backup.

But he couldn't do that.

Because if he did, then Abdel would be left here alone, hundreds of miles from his mother and brother. If social services had ever existed here, then the gaps in the safety net were now as wide as the Pacific. At best, he would end up on the street. At worst...

Trapp shook off the thought.

"You're…" Sikorski said, frowning. "What?"

"Stay here, look after Breyer. The cavalry will be here before you know it. Literally."

"The fuck I am!"

"Yes," Trapp growled. "The fuck you are. You are going to stay here and make sure nothing happens to Breyer. I'll be back by the time the big guns arrive. And if I'm not, you leave without me."

"You're insane…" Sikorski breathed.

"No," Trapp said, shaking his head. He grabbed Omar by the shoulder and started hauling him toward the door. "I've just been that kid. And nobody looked out for me."

"You try and screw me," Trapp said, leaning so close to Omar's face that he could smell the man's putrid breath, "and I won't put a bullet through you. I'll snap your neck. You understand?"

The deal they had made for Breyer's life on the smoking highway by the Iranian border was that Omar would lead Trapp to the safe house in Tolafarush where he'd stashed his son, Abdel, and then Trapp would set him free.

The terms rankled deep in Trapp's breast. He hadn't lied to Sikorski when he said he'd walked in Abdel's shoes. Nor had he lied to Nadia barely a day earlier. Jason Trapp knew implicitly what it was like to be the son of a man who used violence as easily as he did drink or drugs. Now in his early twenties, he knew that his childhood had scarred him deeply. He could never be an ordinary man, never sit behind a desk or work in an office, probably never raise children of his own.

He was just built different.

And years before he'd made the decision that he could either let that realization break him—or be the making of him.

Naturally, he'd chosen the latter.

The safe house was walking distance from the Kurdish militia headquarters, a little less than a mile. It had taken Trapp about fifteen minutes to cover the distance, dressed in local garb that he'd borrowed, somewhat forcefully, from one of the taller militiamen. He would have been quicker without the need to ensure Omar never got an opening to use his weapon.

"Which one?" Trapp said. Omar had insisted only on showing him the area on a map, not the exact street. As insurance.

"There," the man said, pointing at a dark, narrow house with a closed shop front on the bottom floor.

"Am I going to find anyone inside?"

"An old man. I will tell him to release my son. You won't need to harm him."

"Is he armed?" Trapp asked, knowing he would make that determination himself.

Omar nodded.

"Then he better not do anything stupid," Trapp said, his voice low and firm in the darkness.

Omar led him to a door to the right of the shop's shutters. He rapped several times, loud enough to wake half the street. Trapp glanced around, feeling the sensation of eyes on him, though he could not see where from.

He heard shuffling inside the house. It took almost a full minute for the sound to reach the other side of the metal door. Another thirty seconds for a variety of locks and chains to be opened and unhooked.

"Inside," Trapp snapped, pushing Omar into the house the second the door swung open. He didn't wait to see if the man inside was armed. He just knew this wasn't the kind of place he wanted to loiter out in the open.

The old man stumbled, dropping an AK-47 on the ground in the process. Trapp saw that there was no safety on the weapon and breathed a sigh of relief that none of them had accidentally gotten shot. The man raised his voice, his tone vacillating between fear and anger.

"Tell him to shut up," Trapp said, grunting as he kicked the weapon aside. "We'll be out of his hair before he knows it."

Omar whispered something in hushed Arabic. The old guy seemed to get the message because he quickly quieted, though his eyes flashed angrily in the gloom. Trapp was careful not to lose sight of him. The last thing he needed was a bullet in the back.

"Where's the kid?"

Omar gestured wordlessly. Trapp glanced up and saw that a boy was standing at the other end of the narrow hallway. He thought he would recognize him, but that night in the desert had been so dark—and so much else was going on—that it was like he was looking at the child's face for the first time.

"Ask him if he wants to go to his mother," Trapp commanded. He grabbed the old man and pushed him down flat onto the ground, belly first, and quickly cuffed him. His movement was forceful but not rough.

The translation took a couple of seconds. Abdel's eyes widened at the mention of Nadia's name. He glanced warily between Omar and Trapp, perhaps not believing that the American could be trusted.

"I did what you wanted," Omar snapped, dismissively turning away from his son. "Now let me go."

Trapp looked up at Abdel. He tried to make his expression as caring as possible. It wasn't an emotion he had much experience of.

"Let me take you home, kid," he said in English, not trusting his Arabic to convey what he wanted. "You don't need to worry about me. I'm not here to hurt you."

More rapidfire Arabic ensued, one-way traffic from Omar to his son. Abdel cringed at the sound of every word, almost phys-

ically recoiling from his father. Trapp considered putting a
bullet through the back of Omar's head but restrained himself.
He'd given his word, after all.

And besides, the boy had been through enough trauma.

"I will come," Abdel said loudly, in English, enunciating the
words carefully as if remembering how he'd been taught them
in school.

"Then let's go," Trapp said.

"You'll abide by our deal?" Omar asked insistently.

"I've already forgotten about you," Trapp replied.

He turned toward the door, hearing the sound of a car on
the other side of the street. This wasn't an affluent part of town,
so the rumble of an engine was noticeable, especially at this
time of night.

There was a scuffle behind him, then a single gunshot,
impossibly loud in the confined space.

"Shit," Trapp flinched.

He spun around, raising his weapon and preparing to fire at
whatever new threat had presented itself. Another part of his
brain was cataloguing every body part to see where he was
injured.

It took him a couple of moments to realize that he was fine.

Omar was the one with a hole in his stomach. A dinner-
plate sized bloodstain was quickly spreading around bullet
wound. There was no doubt that it was a fatal shot. Maybe a top
hospital back home could have saved him, if he'd had the good
fortune to be assaulted in the hospital's parking lot.

But this was Diyala Governate. In 2007.

Trapp lowered his weapon and let it fall to the sling around
his shoulder. He held up his palms in a calming gesture. "Put
the gun down, Abdel."

The kid's eyes were wide, as if he was appreciating for the
first time what he had just done. His father fell to his knees,

then collapsed face first onto the floor. He was probably already dead.

Abdel's face went ashen with shock. Trapp moved slowly toward him, closed his hand around the stock of the rifle, and gently pulled it out of the boy's numb fingers. He clasped him to his torso and felt hot tears dripping from the child's eyes.

"It's over," he murmured, not knowing whether Abdel could understand him, and not really caring. "Let's go home."

EPILOGUE

"Thanks for coming," Breyer said.

Trapp inclined his head but said nothing in response. He was glad to have helped save the Delta operator's life, but mostly out of professional pride. He had no personal affinity for the man. The truth was, Breyer had always been a bit of an asshole.

But he was alive, and his worst injury was a hell of a headache. His concussion would rule him out of ops for a few weeks, but the word on the street—which meant the gossip Sikorski had passed on—was that he'd suffered no other serious physical ailments.

That was a good thing.

"You know, I feel like a prick," Breyer said.

Trapp considered saying nothing. Most people felt the need to fill a silence. He never had. He was comfortable with situations that most others would find cripplingly awkward. But since the Delta man was lying in a hospital bed with a large white bandage wrapped around his head, he decided to cut the guy some slack.

"There's a first time for everything," he said, keeping his

expression deadpan for several long moments before finally cracking a slight smile.

"Ouch," Breyer winced, holding up his palms. "But I probably deserved that."

"Forget about it," Trapp said. "I'm a big guy."

"No kidding," Breyer replied.

Trapp studied him for a moment. He looked somehow smaller lying in that hospital bed. Not physically, but as though he'd lost some of the bravado and arrogance that had hung off him like a bad smell ever since Trapp first met him.

The Delta operator let his head fall forward a few inches, then drew in a shop breath as if to steady himself. "Look, I just wanted to thank you for saving my life. You went above and beyond, man. If it wasn't for you, I'd probably have a car battery attached to my nuts right now."

Both men shivered at the thought.

I guess we're not so different after all, Trapp mused.

"Any time," Trapp said.

"I know," Breyer replied, looking at Trapp thoughtfully. "You really mean it, don't you? You'd do exactly the same thing again, no matter which of us got snatched. Right?"

Trapp shrugged.

"I've met a lot of bad motherfuckers, Jason. But you're right up there."

Trapp rubbed his neck. He didn't feel exactly awkward, but he knew he didn't want to linger in this situation much longer.

"You just get better, okay?" he said. "We all just want you back on the street."

Breyer laughed out loud. "You're a bad liar, you know that? I guess you're not perfect after all. Nah, I'm done."

Trapp looked at him quizzically. "What do you mean?"

"I'm not going back out there. I've looked through to the other side, and I don't like what I saw." Breyer shook his head sadly. "I'd be a liability on a mission now. I don't trust myself.

And confidence is all an operator has. I can't stand side by side with my buddies knowing I'm the weak link. I told the colonel already. I guess they'll ship me back stateside. Maybe I'll end up an instructor somewhere. I don't really care."

This time, Trapp really did say nothing. He was looking to the other side himself. Maybe seeing a premonition of what he would look like five years from now. Would the job chew him up and spit him out, just like it had the man lying in the hospital bed in front of him?

"Truth is, I've known a while," Breyer continued. "That's probably why I was such an asshole to you." He grinned sheepishly. "Like I thought I was some kind of alpha lion, snarling and roaring just so you knew your place."

"I guess that makes me Simba," Trapp commented.

"You're better than me, Jason. Better than I ever was. You don't talk a big game. Hell, you don't talk at all. You just execute, night after night. Listen, the team's gonna need fresh blood after I'm gone."

Trapp realized that Breyer was talking about him joining Delta. "What if I'm happy where I am?"

Breyer shook his head. "I've known guys like you my entire career. I know you're not fat and happy. It's not in your makeup. I wasn't either, and I was never anything like you. You want to be the best? Prove it."

He coughed and winced at the pain the involuntary action caused him. "Delta won't be slotting ragheads in the desert forever. One day this war will be over. And when it is, the Unit's going to need men like you."

Trapp saw the outright sincerity on the man's face. He found it strangely touching. "I'll think about it."

"Don't just think. Next selection course is in three months. Be there."

FOR ALL THE LATEST NEWS

I hope you enjoyed *Dust Storm*. If you did, and don't fancy sifting through thousands of books on Amazon and leaving your next great read to chance, then sign up to my mailing list and be the first to hear when I release a new book.

Visit - www.jack-slater.com/updates

Keep reading if you want to learn more about the real-life inspiration that led me to write *Dust Storm*...

Thanks so much for reading!

Jack.

AUTHOR'S NOTE

Hi,

As always, thanks for reading *Dust Storm*!

When I wrote the first Jason Trapp novel five years ago, I had no idea that so many people would clamor for me to keep doing so all this time later. It's a real honor to be able to write for you all, and I hope to do so for many years to come.

I actually started this novella – though it ended up almost long enough to be called a full novel – while in Indonesia a couple of years ago. I wanted to take Trapp back to the early years of his career, and see how he operated as part of a team, instead of as a lone operator. The answer is that he does things his way. If you've got this far, I doubt you're surprised...

In reality, Iranian surface-to-air missiles never ended up presenting a major threat to US and allied forces during the occupation of Iraq. But a civilian airliner was shot down over Iraq by exactly the same missile I talked about in Dust Storm in 2004. In the years since, militant groups have paraded their Misagh-1s in front of the world media. And as we see with Iran's Shahed drones and ballistic missiles from Ukraine to the Red

Sea, the regime has no problem funneling advanced weapons to entirely unsavory characters.

I like to think that the reason international airlines are still able to fly over Iraq is down to men like Trapp, working in secrecy for all of our benefit.

The next time you see Trapp will be in an entirely new series, in which he – along with other favorite characters such as Mike Mitchell and Eliza Ikeda – will play cameo roles. I've been writing it for the last few months, and you can expect it in Spring 2024. Don't worry, he will also continue to play the starring role in the Jason Trapp series. I apologize for taking such an uncharacteristically long break between releases, but you can expect to see plenty more of him over the next few months!

Jack.

ALSO BY JACK SLATER

Jason Trapp series in order:

Dark State

False Flag

Flash Point

Depth Charge

The Apparatus

Black Eagle

Valley of Death

Hand of God

Blake Larsen crime series in order:

In The Dark

She Lies Here

Among The Pines

—

Printed in Great Britain
by Amazon

36002663R00108